Tuesday's Child

Clare Revell

Tuesday's Child

Contact Information: titleadmin@pelicanbookgroup.com

All scripture quotations, unless otherwise indicated, are taken from the Holy Bible, New International Version(R) NIV(R) Copyright 1973, 1978, 1984 by Biblica, Inc.™ Used by permission of Zondervan. All rights reserved worldwide. www.zondervan.com

Cover Art by Nicola Martinez

White Rose Publishing, a division of Pelican Ventures, LLC
www.pelicanbookgroup.com PO Box 1738 *Aztec, NM * 87410

White Rose Publishing Circle and Rosebud logo is a trademark of Pelican Ventures, LLC

Publishing History
First White Rose Edition, 2012
Print Edition ISBN 978-1-61116-208-0
Electronic Edition ISBN 978-1-61116-207-3
Published in the United States of America

Monday's Child must hide for protection,
Tuesday's Child tenders direction,
Wednesday's Child grieves for his soul,
Thursday's Child chases the whole,
Friday's Child is a man obsessed,
Saturday's Child might be possessed,
And Sunday's Child on life's seas is tossed,
Awaiting the Lifeboat that rescues the lost.

Dedication

To Grandad.
Deaf for most of his life, we had wonderful
conversations with the white board and marker pen.
Gone but never forgotten.

Thanks to Detective Constable Philip Wilson for the
police procedure advice.

Other Titles by Clare Revell

Praise for Clare Revell

Season for Miracles

This author definitely has talent and great imagination. Kyle and Holly came to life in this book with so much ease they hardly sounded fictional and so real. The pain and fear that Holly goes through is heartbreaking but I loved that with Kyle anything is possible. This is definitely a book worth reading for it has everything just right for the season: God and hope. ~Lena, Happily Ever After Reviews

Saving Christmas

Clare Revell does it again with this beautiful story of hope and redemption. *Saving Christmas* packs a lot of story into a limited number of pages, and draws the reader in from the very first line. It's a wonderful respite from the hectic holiday to-do list. ~Author Mary Manners

Cassie's Wedding Dress

When long-time friends Jack and Cassie reconnect, you think the ride is almost over, but Ms. Revell has a few surprises left in this short, sweet, and emotionally satisfying story. I'll be watching for Clare Revell's next book. Five stars for *Cassie's Wedding Dress*! ~ Author Dora Hiers

Time's Arrow

I stand in awe of Revell's ability to pack an entire novel's worth of action and emotion into so few pages. ~Author Delia Latham

1

Tuesday's Child tenders direction…

*Let your gentleness be evident to all. The Lord is near.
Do not be anxious about anything, but in every situation, by
prayer and petition, with thanksgiving, present your
requests to God. And the peace of God, which transcends all
understanding, will guard your hearts and your minds in
Christ Jesus. Philippians 4: 5-7*

That girl really has no sense of time whatsoever.

Manning the reception desk of Datura Doll
Hospital wasn't Adeline Monroe's idea of fun. She was
more of a hands-on person than a receptionist, and as
soon as Susie returned from her break, Adeline would
be where she belonged—out back mending the
growing pile of dolls and teddy bears. The doll
hospital she ran with her best mate, Jasmine, seemed to
be one of the few businesses on the High Street not
struggling in the current economic climate. She
guessed it was because no one wanted to buy new if
old could be repaired.

Besides, nothing spoke comfort like the teddy
you'd grown up with and shared many a nightmare
and secret with.

Constant rain hit soundlessly against the
windows. So much for the unbroken sunshine and
temperatures of seventy-seven degrees Fahrenheit

predicted for today. Adeline chuckled. Of course the Met Office hadn't forecast the hurricane that had completely devastated the south of England a couple of years ago, either. Hopefully, this storm wouldn't be a repeat. Even if it did mean she no longer had to water the plants when she got home tonight.

Drumming her fingers on the desk, she eyed the clock and sighed. Susie's hour break seemed to get longer each day. "Where is she?"

She glanced down. Ben, her black and white Cavalier King Charles spaniel, sat resting his head on his front paws, one ear cocked open as always. His coat shone, and he opened his mouth in a long lazy yawn before raising his dark, soulful eyes up to her.

"You think Susie's taking a nap somewhere, huh, Ben?" she asked, reaching down and stroking him. "More likely she's run into that boyfriend of hers and lost track of time."

The door flung open letting a blast of wind and rain in with it. Ben jumped up and pushed at Adeline. She acknowledged him by rubbing his ears and then twisted her head to glance over at the door. "Hello."

A small child stood in the doorway, her coat flapping undone and dripping a puddle of rainwater onto the floor. A pale blue bobble hat with woolen braids hanging off the ear flaps was pulled down snugly over her head. Known as 'dappy' hats, they were all the rage.

Adeline even had one hanging on the peg in her hallway.

A doll clutched in her hand, chest heaving, the child stood motionless, her gaze darting around.

I know it's raining, but a wooly hat in the middle of summer? It's not as if it's cold.

"Hello? Can I help you?" Adeline moved around the desk towards her.

"She's broken." The child held out the one-armed doll, tears streaking her face. "It said doll hospital..." She turned her head away, and Adeline missed the last half of the sentence.

"I'm sorry. I need you to face me so I can read your lips. I'm deaf."

The child turned back, staring at her, eyes wide with wonder. "For real? You can't hear anything I say?"

Adeline shook her head. "Nope, but if you look at me when you speak, I can read your lips."

"But you can talk. I thought deaf people only talked with their hands. They didn't have voices 'cause they didn't need them."

Adeline smiled at her, signing as she spoke. It was refreshing to be with someone who said what they thought instead of hiding their reaction. "I can talk with my hands *and* my voice. I could hear just like you can until I was five. So what did you say?"

"I said the sign said doll hospital, but it doesn't look like a hospital. There aren't any beds. And it doesn't have that funny smell."

"Well, when you go to the people hospital are there beds in reception?"

The child wiped her nose on her sleeve and hiccoughed through the tears. "No. I guess not."

"Nor here. What happened to your doll?" Adeline pulled a tissue from the box on the counter and offered it to the sobbing child.

"Uncle Nate broke her."

"I'm sure he didn't mean to."

She nodded her head vigorously. "Yeah, he did."

"What's your name?"

"Don't have one."

Really? I thought everyone had a name. Adeline bit her lip, wondering how she could find out. Maybe deal with the doll first and make friends that way.

"All right. Tell you what. Let's take your doll into the next room and check her over. Does she have a name?" She stood and reached for the peg behind her, pulling her white doctor's coat over her street clothes.

"Her name's Amelia Jane like in the story. Only she's not bad." She scrutinized Adeline's badge. "Doctor...what's that word?"

"That's my name. Dr. Adeline."

"That's a pretty name."

"Thank you. I expect yours is pretty, too."

The child shook her head.

Adeline grabbed a clipboard with forms on it and smiled. "If you come this way, we'll get her on a bed and fill in some paperwork. Then I'll check her over."

She led the way through the side door, Ben by her heels, and grinned at the expression of wonder that came over the child's face. It was the same every time, but she never grew tired of seeing their faces light up on their first view of the hospital she and her father had created.

Doll-sized beds lined the shelves set at chair height along each wall. Each bed contained a doll or teddy with bandages in the appropriate places. Some had miniature IV's set up, while others had tiny oxygen cylinders by the bed. A sign on the wall announced visiting times, and each bed had a vase of flowers on the side table. A chair placed next to each bed ensured any visitor could drop by properly.

"Wow, wow, wow." The child slowly turned

around.

"What do you think?" Adeline asked, unable to read her lips.

The girl grinned at her, eyes like saucers. "It's amazing. Just like the real thing."

"And just like the real thing, I need you to book Amelia Jane in while I examine her. Pop her up on the couch for me. Did you bring her arm?"

"And her finger." The child set the doll gently onto the exam couch and pulled the arm and finger from her pocket, putting them next to the doll. Her hand touched the doll's face, as if she were reassuring her that everything was going to be all right.

Adeline handed the clipboard over and set about her work checking the doll. The crack on the doll's forehead was superficial. A little glue and paint and it would be gone. The arm could be reattached with a new elastic band and the finger would just need a little glue and paint. She glanced up. "How's the form coming on?"

The child handed it back.

"You have lovely handwriting. It's almost as neat as mine." Adeline skimmed it and pointed to a blank line. "You didn't put your name on here where it says next of kin."

"What's that mean?"

"That's the name of the main person who looks after the doll, so we know who to talk to about her and ring when she's better. Usually her mummy or daddy, but not always. I'm guessing that's you, so you need to put your name in there."

"Uncle Nate said never to tell strangers my name."

"Uncle Nate is a very wise man, but I'm not a stranger. I'm Amelia Jane's doctor, and I need to know what to call you." She tilted her head. "I can't call you Amelia Jane's mummy."

"True." She took the clipboard back and, tongue hovering over her bottom lip, painstakingly wrote her name down.

"Vianne Ophelié Holmes. That's a very pretty name. Did I pronounce it right?"

Vianne nodded. "You did. I'm named after mummy. She was Ophelié."

"Well, Vianne, the good news is I can make Amelia Jane better, but you'll have to leave her here for a few days." Adeline ran a finger down the form and did a double take. "Child abuse?"

"I told you. Uncle Nate broke her."

"How did he break her? Did he drop her?"

"No. He said I was too big to play with dolls and put her on top of the wardrobe. I climbed on a chair to get her down, only it was a swivel chair and we fell. She broke, and I hurt my knee and my hand." Tears filled Vianne's eyes again. "It really hurts."

"Let me check you over, as well. Sit up here with Amelia Jane for a moment." Adeline lifted Vianne onto the couch next to the doll.

Now that Vianne knew the doll would be all right, the pain from her own injuries took over.

"Let's have a look. I can be pretty good at fixing bumps and scrapes on people as well."

Vianne pulled up her pant legs, and Adeline checked her over.

"It just needs a plaster and you'll be fine. But a fall isn't child abuse. That's deliberately hurting a child. And neither he nor you did that. This was an accident. So how about we change the form to reflect that?"

A thoughtful expression crossed Vianne's face and

she nodded slowly. "All right. A big fall. Can you make Amelia Jane better with a plaster, too?"

Adeline reached for the first aid kit. "I wish I could, but Amelia Jane hurt herself badly when she fell. She'll need surgery on her arm, head, and finger. So I reckon four days before you can take her home."

"Will she have a bed?"

Adeline opened the box of plasters and offered them to Vianne to choose one. "Of course. And you can come and visit in the afternoons between two and four, except Sunday. We have a selection of books and comics you can read to her."

"Cool. Can you look at her eyes, too? Her left one won't open anymore. Uncle Nate says she's blind 'cause she's so old. She used to be mummy's once."

"Sure I can have a look. It won't take long." Adeline changed the details and added eyes to the clipboard, impressed how Vianne always looked at her as she spoke. That was something most adults tended to forget mid-conversation.

Vianne handed her a bright pink dolphin plaster. "This one."

"Great choice." Adeline fixed it on her knee and jumped her down off the couch. "There you go, all done. Now, you can pick an empty bed for Amelia Jane and put her in it. This card goes in the slot at the end of the bed."

Vianne took the doll and card, and headed across the room. She fussed over the doll as she settled her into the bed and tucked her in.

"Shall I give mummy or daddy a ring to come pick you up?"

"I live with Uncle Nate. He's working until five. It's an inset day—"

"An insect day?"

Vianne laughed, her whole face lighting up. "No, an inset day. It's where the teachers have lessons, and we have a day off. I was supposed to go to Mrs. Sullivan. She lives next door, but Sophie has the measles, and I haven't had them. So Mrs. Sullivan wouldn't let me in. She said I needed to stay away so I didn't get sick, too. I don't like being sick cause it means I have to stay in bed for days and days and days."

Adeline forced a smile as a shiver ran down her spine. That was exactly how she'd lost her hearing. Complications from a high fever she'd contracted with the measles. "I see. Does Uncle Nate know Sophie's sick?"

Vianne shook her head and chewed on a nail. "Nope, he left for work as I knocked on the door. Mrs. Sullivan gave me the spare key so I could get back in the house. I was on my own all day. Even made my own lunch—a jam, marmite and cheese sandwich, crisps, and fizzy pop. I left the back door unlocked so I can get back in."

"Jam, cheese and marmite? Not all together, surely?"

Vianne grinned and nodded. "It's yummy. Not as nice as peanut butter, though."

Adeline wrinkled her nose. "Peanut butter is disgusting. But you're clever to make your own lunch. How old are you?"

"Ten and a half."

She couldn't let the child leave on her own. Who knew what would happen, especially with the serial killer at large? No one was safe. A small child alone would be easy prey.

"You're not really old enough be on your own, and I can't let you back out in this weather. Let me ring Uncle Nate and see what he wants to do."

"I'll be fine at home. He finishes soon, anyway."

She tilted her head. "Actually Uncle Nate will be in big trouble if anyone finds out you were home on your own."

Vianne's face fell. "Oh. I don't want to get him in trouble."

"If it's all right with him, perhaps you can stay here and help man the front desk." She glanced up and saw Susie sitting in her chair now. "I've got a stack of coloring sheets if you're interested."

Vianne nodded. "If Uncle Nate says it's OK. What's your dog called?"

"His name is Benjamin, but I call him Ben." She smiled as Ben's ears pricked up at the mention of his name.

"Benjamin? That's a funny name. But Ben suits him."

"I think so, too. How do I get hold of Uncle Nate?"

"He's a policeman." Vianne shoved her hand into her pocket and pulled out a small card. "Here's his number."

Adeline smiled, picked up the phone and started to dial.

A small hand touched her arm. "You're deaf. How do you use the phone?"

"It's a special one. You just watch."

****

Detective Sergeant Nate Holmes swung his chair back on two legs and glared at the file in his hand. He flicked it closed and then looked over at his partner, DS Dane Philips. "I hate paper trails. Especially this one." He tossed the file onto his desk and picked up another one. "It doesn't matter which way I look at it, or how long and hard I pray about it, it's going nowhere fast. If we had time it wouldn't matter, but we don't. Every second he's still out there, women are at risk."

Dane peered at him over thick-rimmed reading glasses. "Tell me about it. The victims don't even have the same eye or hair color. Nor are they in the same age bracket—this guy isn't choosy. Once we find the link then maybe we'll get a lead on him."

"The press is calling him the Herbalist. As the name of every road he's struck in is named after an herb. He may not be striking in alphabetical order, but so far we've had Parsley, Ragwort, and Onion."

"Herbalist. I guess it's as good a name as any. It also fits with the plants left on the bodies. It's interesting he picks the same ones as the road names. He obviously has a strange sense of humor. Either that or he's sending a weird message."

Nate laughed as Dane scrawled 'Herbalist' over the front of the file. He snatched up the phone as it rang. "DS Holmes."

"Sgt. Holmes, my name is Adeline Monroe. I run the doll hospital on the High Street."

The voice was muffled, and Nate struggled to place the accent. He shook his head at the coffee mug Dane waved at him. He put a hand over the phone. "No, thanks, I drink anymore today and I'll drown." He lifted his hand again. "How can I help you, Miss Monroe?"

"I have Vianne here with me. She came in on her own about forty minutes ago."

The chair slammed back onto all four legs, Nate's attitude changing. His heart pounded. He'd left Vianne with Mrs. Sullivan. What was she doing out on her own? He glanced at the window at the storm raging outside. "Is she all right? She's not hurt, is she?"

"She has a small scrape on her knee, which I patched up. Other than that she's fine. Amelia Jane, on the other hand, needs a little more fixing up."

A tight sigh escaped him as he pinched the bridge of his nose tightly. *That wretched doll. How'd she find it?* He didn't need this today. "Have Mrs. Sullivan pick her up—I can give you her number…"

"Apparently Sophie has the measles. Vianne's been home alone all day."

How much worse could the day get? "Great. All right I'll come get her as soon as I can arrange cover here." Nate tossed the file to the desk.

"I'm more than happy for her to stay here until you finish work. She can sit in main reception and color."

"I don't want to impose."

"You're not."

"All right, thank you. I'll be there as soon after five as I can." He flung the receiver down and pushed a hand through his hair. "That's all I need."

"What's up?" Dane looked at him.

"Sophie's sick, so Vianne has evidently been home alone all day. She somehow managed to get that wretched doll off the top of the wardrobe and broke it. She took it to the doll hospital on the High Street."

"I know it well, mate. That's where Jasmine works."

"Then you'll know the owner, Adeline Monroe?"

Dane nodded. "We've been friends with Adeline

for years. She's deaf, but never let it hold her back."

Nate looked at the phone. "Deaf? I just spoke with her on the phone."

Dane laughed. "She has a phone that goes through an operator. She talks, you reply, and she gets what you said as a text message. It's a really clever system."

"I'm sure."

"Hey, don't knock it until you've tried it."

"I just did, didn't I?"

A cough from the door drew Nate's attention towards it. His boss, Detective Inspector Vanessa Welsh, stood there, short dark hair framing her face and piercing blue eyes clouded with grief—something he'd seen all too often in recent days. A sharp stab hit him hard in the stomach. *Not again.*

"Guv?"

"Nate, you and Dane need to get over to Tamarisk Crescent. Body of a young girl in her late teens has been found."

"On our way." Nate stood, sending his chair flying backwards. Reigning in his grief and anger, he sent up a prayer for the latest victim and her family. He grabbed his coat and shrugged into it. "We need to catch this creep, Dane."

"Tell me something I don't know. I was hoping that you being a church elder meant you had some pull with the Bloke upstairs. You know, maybe He'd give you some hints as to who this guy is."

"I wish. I have prayed so hard about this. Even asked Pastor Jack to pray about it." Their footsteps echoed on the stairs as they ran down. "Guess He is waiting for me to do some of the leg-work first." Nate pulled his collar up against the rain. "So what's she like?"

"What's who like?"

"This deaf lady I'm trusting to look after my niece."

"Adeline is blonde, blue eyes, lovely girl…not slim by any stretch of the imagination, but who wants a slim woman anyway? And best of all, she goes to Headley Baptist."

"She does?"

Dane unlocked the car and slid into the driver's seat of the pool car allocated to them. "She sits downstairs with her hearing dog, Ben. He's a gorgeous black and white King Charles spaniel."

Nate slammed the door and fastened his seat belt. "Hmmm. You'll be telling me next she's single."

"She is, actually. Maybe we can get the two of you together—"

"Forget it. I'm not interested in a relationship. I keep telling you that. I just wanted to make sure she hasn't got a record."

Dane started the car, flipping on lights and wiper blades. "She doesn't. And I'll keep trying. Not all women are like your sister-in-law."

"Pete died because of Ophelié. Because of me. If I hadn't told him where she was, he'd never have gone to France. They wouldn't have been on the plane when it crashed."

"It was an accident."

"We'll have to agree to disagree there. Are we going, or what?"

"We're going."

****

Just before five thirty, Ben tapped Adeline's ankle

with his paw.

"What's up?" She watched him run to the office door, and got to her feet. That meant there was someone out there she needed to see. She followed him into main reception.

A tall man with light brown, spiky hair stood there, his arms wrapped around Vianne as he lifted her off the floor in a bear hug. His blue eyes filled with sorrow as he looked the child over, making sure she really was all right. One hand held her tightly, the other patted the hat she still wore.

Adeline angled herself so she could read both sets of lips.

"Hey, pumpkin."

"Are you cross with me, Uncle Nate?"

"Well…"

"I've been really good. I couldn't go to Sophie's house because she's sick. I made lunch and put the things in the washdisher afterwards. And I didn't use the oven because you said not to if you weren't there."

"Dishwasher," Nate corrected.

"Dishwasher," Vianne repeated. "This is Dr. Adeline. She's fixing Amelia Jane and this is Ben. He's her special hearing dog."

Nate put Vianne down and held out a hand to Adeline. "DS Holmes. Pleased to meet you, Miss Monroe. I'm sorry I'm later than I originally said. Something cropped up in the case I'm working."

Adeline shook his hand. His cool grip was firm, and she watched his gaze size her up. He was gorgeous. His full lips moved almost in slow motion, and she wondered for a moment what it would be like to feel them on hers.

I've read way too many romance novels in which many

of the heroines have a size eight figure with hardly a flaw in sight. In the old days, women over thirty were like me, spinsters, chunky and a size sixteen. Top heavy and pear shaped. How can I compete with that? Kind of hard to like the way I look with all the supermodels in the papers and magazines.

She dragged her thoughts back to the man in front of her and the reason he was here. Collecting his niece. "And you, Sergeant. And please don't worry about the time. You have an important job." Somehow she managed to get her voice to work.

"Thank you for looking after Vianne. I'm sorry if she was a bother."

"She was as good as gold. Not a bother at all."

Nate turned and looked at Vianne and spoke quickly, his face angled so Adeline couldn't see what he said.

Vianne scowled at him and stomped over to a chair by the door.

Nate faced Adeline again. "How much do I owe you for the doll?"

"I'll do you an invoice. We open the ward for the children to visit between two and four every afternoon bar Sunday." She shuffled the papers on the reception desk. "I could have the invoice ready for you by tomorrow, once I've had a proper look at the doll. I'll ring when she can go home. It should be around three to four days, to allow the glue time to set and for the paint to dry properly."

Movement from the door caught her eye. She glanced behind Nate to see Vianne waving at him. "…we come visit, please, Uncle Nate?"

A shadow filled his eyes as he gazed at Vianne. When he turned back, Adeline realized she'd missed part of what he was saying. "…taken up enough of your time. Thank you again." He moved to the door.

Vianne got to her feet and took his outstretched hand. She looked directly at Adeline as she spoke. "Thank you for having me, and thank you for fixing my knee, and for looking after Amelia Jane."

Adeline smiled. "You're welcome." The light flashed to signify the door opening and as it closed, she looked down at Ben. "Well, I guess he had a bad day at work. He never seems that sad or grumpy in church."

Jasmine came into reception, pulling on her coat. She looked at Adeline, signing as she spoke. "Everything's locked up tight. Was that Nate Holmes I just heard?"

"Yes." Adeline signed rapidly in response. "How do you know him?"

"Other than from church, he's Dane's partner. He's also one of the elders. You've seen him serving communion, just probably never realized he's a cop. It's not something he tends to advertise. Is everything all right?"

"Everything's fine. He came to pick Vianne up. You know, she didn't take the hat off once, despite it being soaking wet."

"That doesn't surprise me. I've never seen her without a hat."

"What about school?"

"No idea, have to ask Jodie. They're in the same form. Hey, what are you doing Sunday?"

Adeline thought for a moment. "Nothing as far as I know."

"Come with us for dinner after church."

"I'd love that. I'll bring dessert. See you tomorrow."

"Sure, but no dessert. I've got that covered. Night." Jasmine opened the door and headed into the fine drizzle.

Adeline reached down and petted Ben. "Shall we go home?" She smiled as he licked her hand. "I wonder what made Sgt. Holmes so sad. We'll pray for him tonight, see if that helps."

She shivered as something touched her heart, a heaviness she knew all too well—a pressing need to pray for the man who just left. A burden that wouldn't wait until later, and a heaviness that wouldn't lift until she'd done what the Lord wanted. Locking the front door, Adeline turned back towards her office, not knowing what to pray, just knowing she had to and had to do so now.

2

Saturday, unlike the day before, was blistering hot. Even with the fan on and the windows wide open, Adeline's shirt was damp and sticking to her overheated skin. She was what her grandmother called a grease spot. *Oh, the joys of an English summer, where you dress for the day and not for the season.*

Ben lay under the desk, panting hard, despite the bowl of water by his side. He still managed to tap her foot as the door opened.

Adeline leaned down and patted his head, and then looked up. She smiled a welcome. "Hi."

Vianne skipped across reception to the desk, the pink and white striped dappy hat pulled down over her ears, braids swinging on either side. "Hello, Dr. Adeline. We've come to visit Amelia Jane."

"Sure. Susie will show you through." She smiled as Vianne tugged free of her uncle's hand and skipped after Susie. Adeline turned her attention to Nate. Dressed in a simple white tee shirt and beige slacks, he looked even more handsome than he had yesterday in his suit, tie and overcoat. Shivers ran down her spine, and her heart flip-flopped.

"Would you like some coffee while she's visiting?"

"Coffee would be great, thank you. I have two sugars, no milk, please. And the invoice, if you have it done."

"I did it this morning." Adeline pulled it from the

drawer and handed it to him.

Nate glanced down the sheet, his lips moving as he read.

Adeline kept her smile to herself, knowing he hadn't intended her to pick up on his immediate thoughts.

His head jerked up and his gaze held hers. "Her eyes?"

Adeline nodded. "Vianne asked me to look at them as the doll was blind. They were easy to fix. They'd simply come unattached."

"Oh, right. It's a very old doll, belonged to her mother when she was a child." He looked down again. "Do I pay now or…?"

"When you pick her up is fine." She turned her attention to pouring the coffee.

His scent overpowered even the strong coffee she loved. He smelled of musk and spearmint. Did he know how captivating it was? Every nerve ending tingled with his nearness. She glanced down as Ben touched her foot, then back to Nate.

"…place is set up."

Extrapolating quickly, Adeline guessed what he was asking. "I'll give you a tour if you like." She offered him the mug.

"Thank you. That would be great."

Adeline led him through the door to the right. "Most of our work is done here. As you can see it's laid out as you'd expect a workshop to be. Sometimes we have to order in parts, but most of them we have here already."

Nate glanced around. "How long has it been here?"

"We've been on the High Street about a year. We

moved from the original site in Datura Drive where we'd been since Dad started it thirty years ago. I've been running the place four years, since Dad retired." She pushed open another door. "And this is the ward."

Nate's expression became one of amazement much the same way Vianne's had the day before as he glanced around. "Well, you certainly have lots of patients, Miss Monroe. Or should that be Dr. Monroe?"

"Dad always used Doctor for the kids, since we were making their toys better. It seemed natural for me to do the same thing. But I prefer Dr. Adeline or Dr. A."

Nate sipped the coffee. "I owe you an apology for the way I spoke to you yesterday."

"Don't worry about it. I put it down to a bad day in the office."

Nate nodded. "It wasn't one of the best. But that's no excuse for being rude. I should know better. I'm sorry."

"You're forgiven. I prayed for you last night."

He looked completely gobsmacked. "You...you did?"

"I always pray for the pastors and elders, but last night God laid you on my heart, especially."

"Thank you." His eyes softened, making a huge difference to his face. "I appreciate it."

She smiled at him. "You're welcome."

Nate walked with her to the office.

"So how do you manage if you can't hear?"

"I read lips and sign."

"How come you speak so well?"

"I got the measles when I was five and lost my hearing, then. My mother insisted I carried on speaking and learned both lip reading and sign. She made the whole family learn. But Ben is my best asset." She glanced at her faithful friend by her heels. "He's my hearing dog. He tells me when the phone rings or the doorbell chimes or when the smoke alarm goes off. Or when someone wants my attention, and I haven't noticed them."

"So a guide dog for the deaf, then?"

"Yes. I'd be lost without him. He's two now. I've had him six months."

Nate settled into the chair by her desk, his long legs stretched out. One hand rested on his thighs, the other held his coffee. He fixed his gaze on her, a long lazy smile curving his full lips. "I don't remember the last time I just sat and did nothing."

"You should do it more often."

"Bit hard in my line of work. Especially with the case I'm currently involved in." He took a long drink. "There are no leads, just—" He broke off. "You don't want to hear this."

"If you want to talk, I'm happy to listen." She smiled, waiting for him to catch the little joke.

It took him a second. He grinned, at ease, and then his expression sobered. He took a long drink of his coffee, indecision playing over his face. "Thanks, but I really shouldn't. It's an ongoing investigation."

"All right. I'll keep praying. And if you should change your mind, I'm here."

"Thank you." He ran his fingers around the rim of the cup. "Have you done any kind of self-defense classes?"

"I have Ben."

Nate took in the way Ben sat by her heels. "And as fierce as he is, a backup plan might be an idea. I run a self-defense course in the church hall on Monday evenings at seven. You'd be welcome to join us."

"Thank you. I'll think about it."

Nate finished his coffee. "I should take Vianne home. I have a thousand and one things to do around the house today. Thanks for the coffee. And the prayers, Miss Monroe."

Adeline smiled. "You're welcome, Sgt. Holmes."

He got to his feet, his tall frame not in the least bit imposing. "I'll see you tomorrow."

For a moment her heart leapt, then she realized he meant in church and a shaft of disappointment filled her. "We'll be there."

****

Walking down the aisle to her usual seat in Headley Baptist, Adeline was amused to see that Ben adopted his church attitude almost as soon as they entered the building and walked sedately. She smiled at Holly and Kyle and said hello as she passed them. They really did make a beautiful couple. Who'd have thought God could work such a horrid situation for good the way He had with them?

She slid into the pew and Ben settled at her feet.

Chrissie and Matt sat in front of her. They'd announced their engagement only recently. It seemed as if the church would soon have a spate of weddings.

Glancing down the order of service, her attention was diverted by a hand on her arm. She looked up into a pair of bright eyes and beaming smile under a wooly hat. This time the dappy hat was florescent yellow. "Hey, Vianne."

"Can we come and sit with you?"

"Sure. Mind you don't trip over Ben."

"I won't."

Adeline swung her legs to the side so Vianne and Nate could move past her. She got a delicious aroma of musk and spearmint as Nate brushed past—the small touch of his legs on her knees sending a blast of heat through her. *Really, in church, too* she scolded herself.

He smiled as he sat and her insides followed her heart in a storm of butterflies and thudding.

Anyone would think I was twelve. She smiled back. "How are you, Vianne?"

"I'm OK," Vianne replied making sure to look at her. "How do you say that in sign?"

Adeline showed her. "This is 'how are you?' This is 'I'm well' or 'I'm sick'." She smiled as Vianne copied the signs flawlessly. "Very good," she said, signing as she spoke.

Vianne tilted her head slightly. "So, how does this work? When you can't hear what's happening?"

"I read the lips of whoever is speaking in the pulpit, and I can feel the music."

"Feel the music?" she repeated, her eyes widening.

"Yes. The sound the organ makes sends vibrations though the air. And if I watch Pastor Jack, I can see when he's singing, so I know when to start if it's one I know."

"That's clever. Does Ben tell you, too?"

"He puts his paw on my foot when it's time to stand and sing, but as everyone else stands then, it's easy to figure out."

Nate tapped Vianne's arm. "Shh, now."

Adeline turned her attention to the front, following Pastor Jack's words relatively easily. It was a standing joke between them that even if the PA system failed, he'd have to carry on preaching as she'd be able to tell what he was saying even if no one else could hear him.

After Vianne left for Sunday School, Nate slid up the pew next to her, and she found herself overwhelmed by his clean scent and aftershave.

Lord, help me here. I am meant to be worshipping You, not acting like some teenager with a crush because some man...a very handsome man...is sitting next to me. I can feel my cheeks burning. Maybe I should have worn something else. I look like mutton dressed as lamb. What must he think? Just listen to me going on like this.

Ben knocked his paw against her foot, and she stood with everyone else for the hymn.

Keep my mind focused, Lord, and if it does wander again, then I'll pray for him. She stood with the others, reciting the words of the hymn in her head, aware of Nate's hand inches from hers. For a moment she wondered what it would be like to have a man hold her hand in church, the way Matt had just grabbed Chrissie's, or to have someone look at her with love.

So many of her friends and people around her had found their soul mate now, that she couldn't help but wonder if there was someone out there for her. Someone like Nate, who wasn't just outwardly handsome, although he was undeniably good looking, he shone with an inner beauty that came from loving the Lord. If she ever found love, it had to be with someone who shared her faith.

Adeline managed to keep her mind focused on the sermon, which she knew was entirely thanks to the Lord and nothing to do with her. She was far too easily distracted when left to her own devices. Keeping her eyes on Pastor Jack until the benediction finished, she sat down and closed her eyes, a heavy burden coming over her again.

Why did she feel so led to pray for Nate? Surely it wasn't simply the fact that he was sitting next to her? Or was it? His presence filled her senses, but as she prayed, the burden she felt eased and the peace of the Lord descended like a dove.

Lifting her head, she found Ben curled in her lap, concern in his eyes. Had she been that engrossed in prayer she hadn't noticed him jump up? "I'm fine," she told him, petting his ears. Long, slim fingers touched hers and she followed the arm to Nate's worried face. Fire radiated from his touch, sending ripples of warmth throughout her body.

"Are you all right?" Anxiety filled his eyes.

"I'm fine. Why?"

Nate waved his hand and Adeline glanced around, suddenly realizing the church was empty apart from the two of them. She looked back at him.

"...on the verge of calling an ambulance."

Confusion filled her as there was no one around. "Who needs an ambulance?"

"Pastor Jack was going to call one for you in a few more minutes. First we thought you were sleeping, then unconscious, but Ben didn't seem unduly concerned."

"Oh." Heat flamed in her cheeks and nausea filled her. "I didn't mean to worry everyone."

A waft of aftershave and movement from the pew in front made her turn. "Pastor Jack, I'm so sorry to cause such a fuss."

His grey-green eyes sparkled with a hint of concern. "As long as you're all right, then it's not a problem. Neither is calling someone to check you over."

"I'm fine. It's just as soon as you finished the benediction, this huge burden for prayer came over me, and I just had to give in to it. I didn't realize I was praying so long though."

Pastor Jack smiled. "Time spent with the Lord is never time wasted. Especially when it's a response to something He's telling you to do. I'm glad you're all right. I'll see you tonight."

Adeline nodded. "I should go. Jasmine will be wondering where I am."

Nate touched her arm. "I said I'd bring you. She's taken Vianne already."

"I don't want to put you out."

"You're not. She asked us over for the day. She said you were coming as well, and suggested I bring you and Ben."

"Did she now?" That sounded suspiciously like Jasmine-the-Matchmaker at work.

Nate tilted his head. "Is that a problem? Did you not want to leave your car here?"

"Ben and I walked this morning. I was thinking more of him getting hair on your car seats."

Nate petted Ben. "It's not a problem. He doesn't look like he sheds much anyway. Shall we go?"

Adeline got to her feet, grasping the pew in front as her knees buckled. A strong sense of foreboding closed in on her. *Not again…*

Her vision danced, and a red sheen dropped over her sight. For a moment she saw a teenager, blonde hair tied in a ponytail, sitting on a swing, laughing, playing, safe. Then the next moment the same girl, wearing a red sweater, lay on her stomach in the mud, her face to one side with eyes closed, and mouth drawn back in a long silent scream.

A strong hand gripped her arm, jerking her back to reality. Everything spun and she kept her eyes closed until the need to cry passed.

She hated these visions. The first couple had been dreams. Horribly accurate nightmares that left her pinned to the sheets, and terrified to sleep. Now they impinged on her every day activity. At least she'd been able to hide the one at work yesterday.

Lord, God, be with the girl's family. Comfort them in their grief. Give the police the skills they need to catch her killer quickly, before he strikes again.

More than anything else, she hated the fact the visions were always right. This was the fifth. That meant a fifth girl had died.

But if she said something, or went to the police, she'd be branded insane, a fool. It wasn't as if she ever saw the killer's face. She didn't understand why God was showing her these things when she was unable to change the outcome.

"I'm all right," she said once the spinning stopped. She shot Nate a faint smile. "I'm just stiffer than I realized, and a little dizzy."

She wasn't fooling him.

His eyes narrowed and something flashed across his face. He recognized lies. "Are you sure? If you'd rather go home, I can drive there just as easily."

"Really, I'm fine. I can't let Jasmine down. Not after she's gone to all the trouble to cook." She shook her head, trying to clear the images from her mind. She closed her eyes for a long moment then took a deep breath. Walking to Jasmine's wasn't an option, and as he was offering a ride, and going the same way, it would be silly to refuse. "A lift would be good, thank you."

He nodded. "Come on then. It's not too far a walk to where I parked, or I can bring the car around."

Not wanting to appear weak in front of this gorgeous man, Adeline smiled at him. "I'm fine. Really...the fresh air will help."

"All right." Taking her arm, Nate led her down the aisle.

Tempted for a moment to shrug him off, Adeline soon realized that she wouldn't make it two steps without his help.

****

Nate glanced at Adeline as he waited for the traffic lights to change. She had her eyes shut, and he took the opportunity to study her in some detail. She wasn't like most women his older brother, Pete, had tried setting him up with over the years. Pete had preferred brunettes and seemed to think everyone else did too.

However Nate preferred what he termed a 'real woman'. One with curves and a natural, inner beauty. Just like Adeline. She almost shone at times, yet had a sense of vulnerability about her that tugged at his heart strings. If it wasn't for the fact he wasn't interested in a relationship, he'd probably ask her to dinner.

And what's stopping you from doing that? It doesn't have to be a date, just a 'thank you for taking care of Vianne' dinner. And take Vianne, too. Don't want to give Miss Monroe the wrong idea. We could go to the burger place on the High Street. Or I could cook for her. Make something Vianne will eat without a fuss.

And then there was her hearing—or lack thereof. It was somewhat disconcerting knowing she couldn't hear him. If—and that was a big if—he or any other bloke got involved with her, how would that work in the dark? He couldn't whisper sweet nothings in her ear as they danced, or stand behind her like his father did his mother when she was looking out of the window and talk to her.

Adeline opened her eyes and smiled.

He returned the smile and turned back to the road, his cheeks heating at getting caught staring at her. She really was a beautiful woman. Her love for the Lord emphasized it.

Unlike like his sister-in-law. As thin as a rake and made up to the nines, Ophelié had used her feminine charms and beauty on his brother like a spider wove a web, drawing him in and trapping him, before devouring him.

No, women were not to be trusted. They captured your heart, and then broke it. After all, Miss Monroe lied to him in church after that dizzy spell. Insisting she was fine, when it was blatantly obvious she wasn't. He'd have a quiet word with Jasmine. Maybe Miss Monroe would be more akin to talking to her than to him.

Adeline shifted in her seat. "Penny for them."

"For what?"

"Your thoughts. Your eyes clouded over for a moment."

She's perceptive, I'll give her that.

"I was thinking about my brother."

"Is he Vianne's father?"

"Yeah." Nate pulled up at a stop sign.

"She said she lives with you. She hardly mentioned her parents at all."

"My brother and his wife died in a plane crash when Vianne was three. She doesn't really remember them. Pete made me her guardian in his will." He released the handbrake and pulled away.

"I'm sorry. Were you and your brother close?"

Nate tried to stifle the sudden rush of emotion speaking about Pete brought him. "Yeah. I can't say it's been easy, because it hasn't." His voice came out gruffer than he wanted and wracked with grief. For a moment he was glad she couldn't hear him. Now if he could only keep the emotion off his face.

"Must be hard, bringing her up alone."

"Because I'm a cop?"

Adeline shook her head, color touching her cheeks, only accentuating her looks. "No, I didn't say that. Or mean it. I meant not having anyone to share the joy and pain of bringing up a child with."

Nate took a deep breath. "It's hard. I don't know the first thing about what girls like. Never had a sister, it was just me and Pete. I didn't even realize Pete had wanted me to be her guardian until—"

What was it about her that made him open his heart to her like this? He barely knew her, yet this was the second time in two days he almost told her something he'd never told anyone.

"Until?" she asked, a tender tone in her voice he wasn't expecting.

Nate looked back at the road, his eyes burning with the tears he was holding back. He angled his head towards her, so she could read his lips. "I never knew what he saw in Ophelié. He met her on holiday in Paris and was enamored with her. She was a model, more like a painted doll than anything else. She played on the fragility he assigned her. Vianne was born early, about four months before their first wedding anniversary. Pete doted on her."

"She's a very pretty child."

"Like her mother." Nate took a deep breath and pushed a hand though his hair, surreptitiously wiping his eye at the same time. "I was working undercover one night and discovered Ophelié was having an affair. After a lot of heart searching and praying, I finally told Pete. He and Ophelié fought and she left him and moved in with her lover. She left Vianne with Pete."

Nate looked studiously at the road as he drove. He didn't want to see her expression on her face as she watched him speak. If anything it was more than slightly unnerving, knowing she was constantly watching him the whole time. Did he study people in the interrogation room the same way?

"That must have been hard on all of you."

"It was. After six weeks, Pete asked me to find her. I traced her to Paris, and Pete left Vianne with me while he flew over to talk to her."

Nate's voice wobbled and he took a deep breath. "He...he rang from the airport. Said they'd sorted things out and were coming home on the Concorde. I thought I was helping by telling him where she was. Instead I sent him to his death. The Concorde crashed, killing everyone on board."

He pulled over outside Dane and Jasmine's and yanked hard on the handbrake, hearing the gears click against the ratchet as the car shuddered to an abrupt halt. He covered his face with his hands for a moment, desperate to regain control before seeing Vianne.

Images of the flaming plane filled his mind. Hitting debris on the runway as she took off, the Concorde had burst into flames, staying airborne for only a few minutes before crashing onto a hotel just outside of Paris. The horrifying images caught on camera by a passing car, had flashed around the world almost instantly.

Hot tears spilled down his cheeks, and his shoulders shook. *Please, Lord, not now. I don't want to deal with this again. Especially not in front of someone I hardly know.*

"I'm sorry," Adeline said. "I remember seeing the pictures of the Concorde crash on the television."

He blew out a breath, wiped his eyes and turned in his seat towards her. "Vianne doesn't know the reason her parents were on that plane, and she never will. She remembers very little from that time, and that's the way I need it to stay."

"She won't find out from me."

"Thank you."

Adeline reached into her bag and pulled out a packet of tissues. Extracting one, she held it out to him. "Here you go."

Nate smiled gratefully and took it. "Thank you." The irony wasn't lost on him as he used it and then put it in his coat pocket. "I'm sorry."

"Don't apologize. It's fine." She smiled with sympathy in her eyes. "We should probably go in. Jasmine will be wondering where we are."

"Yes…Miss Monroe…thank you."

"You're welcome, Sergeant."

Nate exited the car and opened the back door for Ben to jump out. The dog obediently sat on the pavement waiting for his mistress to get him. He started up the path with her, just as Dane flung open the door and ran towards them.

Nate's stomach sank into his shoes. "What's wrong?"

"We got to go. Jas will keep some dinner for us

and watch Vianne."

"Go where? We're not on duty."

Dane's expression seared him to the core. He only spoke two words, but those two words spoke volumes. "Euphorbia Way." He looked at Adeline. "We'll see you later."

Leaving Adeline on the path, Nate headed back to the car, praying hard that this time the Herbalist would leave them something a little more substantial to go on. "My car is faster than yours. We'll take mine to the station and pick up a pool car. "

"Are you tanking it?" Dane asked.

"Legally tanking it," Nate said looking at him, not even the speeding joke gaining a smile this time. "Would you pray while I drive?"

"Sure, partner."

"Thanks." Nate glanced across at the mirrors and pulled away, heading towards the station before going on to crime scene number five.

****

Still in two minds as whether to go to the self-defense class or not, Adeline tugged her baggy tee-shirt down over her knee length jogging pants. "Do I look all right in this? Or is it too tight?"

Ben put a paw over his nose.

"Thanks for the vote of confidence. I know I don't look great. But we can't all have a wonderfully proportioned figure like Jas, unfortunately. Mind you, it'd be nice to be able to eat what I like without worrying about piling on the calories."

Her gaze fell on the newspaper lying on the table. A blonde girl with blue eyes smiled at her. The same girl she'd seen in the latest 'vision'. The same girl who died at the hands of the man the press called the Herbalist—the latest of five women all strangled by a man who vanished without a trace each time.

Adeline let out a deep shuddering breath. She'd seen each girl just before their death. At least that's what she assumed, as the clothing the papers described matched what she'd seen. She hadn't even told Jasmine about the visions, because she'd insist on her telling Dane. Maybe she should. Then again she didn't want to be laughed out of the police station. But five women had died now. Maybe she should just chance it and say something to Sgt. Holmes tonight or when he brought Vianne to collect Amelia Jane.

Ben appeared with his leash and Adeline smiled. "Yes, all right, we'll go now." She clipped on his leash and slung her bag sideways across her body. Leaving the house, she headed down the street towards the church. Both she and Ben loved walking and it made sense to do that rather than use the car—unless it was pouring with rain.

There were around fifteen ladies of various ages in track suits standing in the church hall when she arrived. Ben settled on the floor by her bag, his wide eyes watching her. His tail thudded on the floor, a sure sign he was content. She signed to him to stay.

She turned around and smiled seeing Rachel. Also deaf and able to speak, Rachel taught sign language but the two of them usually conversed totally in sign.

"Hey," she signed. "How are you?"

Rachel hugged her and then signed rapidly. "I'm good. How are you?"

"Not sure I should be here."

"Why's that? You look good. Ready for action."

Adeline rolled her eyes. "I look frumpy compared to everyone else. You look great in your tracksuit. Not sure I'm cut out for this."

"This old thing?" Rachel dragged her hands down her clothes before signing a response. "You're fine in what you have on."

"I shouldn't have come. I'll take Ben home."

"Please stay. All we do is try to throw Nate on the floor. We don't succeed, but we try and we always have a laugh." She paused. "There's coffee and cake afterwards."

"Like I need cake," Adeline protested, patting her stomach. "These trousers barely fit as it is."

"So pretend they shrank in the wash and buy new ones. It's what I do."

Adeline smiled. From the corner of her eye, she saw Nate come in. He looked gorgeous in his jogging pants and close fitting tee. It showed every line of his chest off to perfection. He caught her gaze and shot her a beaming smile. Her heart thudded and her breath hiked.

Rachel nudged her. "You all right?"

"Fine, why?"

"You're blushing. You like him?"

"He wouldn't give me a second look, so what's the point?" Glad Nate couldn't understand a word of their conversation, Adeline changed the subject. "I think he's ready to start."

Nate glanced around the group. "Good evening ladies. I'll start with a basic recap for those joining us for the first time tonight. The main aim of this class is to teach you how to remain safe on the streets. Carry your bag sideways across your body and under your coat if you can. Always have a phone with you if you have one. Yes, I'll be teaching you how to defend yourself if an assailant comes up to you. But the most important thing is avoid the situations where you might be in danger in the first place."

Adeline watched his lips. He was speaking very fast, but she managed to catch most of what he said. She raised a hand to get his attention. "Avoid them how?"

"If you're on your own, and see something or someone shady or drunk, or a group of rowdy youths, for example, cross the road to avoid them. Or step into a shop. If you can't cross the road or avoid them, pull out your phone and ring someone, anyone or pretend to make a call."

She nodded. "Thank you."

Nate smiled. "Welcome. Now we'll move on to a few basic moves if someone does surprise you. Daphne, care to be my victim?"

Daphne nodded and made her way to the center of the room. Adeline watched as Nate explained how to stamp on the attackers instep and then twist, bringing an elbow down sharply into his groin.

"You should also use your head. If someone puts an arm around your throat and hand over your mouth, bite hard, and then shove your head back as far and hard as you can. Ninety-nine percent of the time they will then relax their grip enough for you to break free. And if you kick them as well, you should have time to run. Scream and shout at the same time, draw as much attention to what is happening to you as you can."

Nate glanced around the room. "Miss Monroe, would you like to try?"

Adeline pointed to her chest. "Me?"

He smiled. "Unless there is another Miss Monroe,

yes, I mean you."

Adeline moved onto the mats. He stood in front of her. "Now I'm going to come up behind you. I know you won't hear me until my arm goes around your throat, but that's fine. Just do exactly what you've been shown. And remember to use your head."

"I'll try."

"Good girl. Turn around."

Adeline turned around, tensing as she stood there. She glanced over at Rachel, who signed 'don't look so scared' at her. She smiled faintly. An arm went around her throat choking her, and another arm grabbed her waist. Panic filled her and everything she'd been taught went out of her mind. She struggled hard, seeing Ben leap to his feet and come running across.

She brought her left foot up sharply against Nate's shin and then stomped on his foot. At the same time she flung her head back as hard and fast as she could, feeling something crunch as she did so.

Nate let go and staggered backwards.

Adeline stood there wondering why everyone else in the class looked horrorstruck. Nausea flooded her. What had she done? She turned around to see Nate sitting on the floor. His face was bright red, his eyes glistened, and blood poured from his nose like a never-ending flood.

3

Nate pulled the car off onto the road.

Vianne's reflection shifted in the car seat behind him. She inspected him from under the brim of his fisherman's hat she'd insisted on wearing. "So tell me again how you broke your nose, Uncle Nate."

Nate studied her in the driving mirror. "You know very well, pumpkin."

Vianne giggled. "In a self-defense class, but you didn't tell me who did it. Was it one of your little old ladies who couldn't say 'boo' to a goose?"

Nate's cheeks burned, and he looked back at the road, not wanting to see his bright red reflection in the mirror or the huge white bandage across his nose. "Something like that," he muttered. "Now you have to promise me that you'll let me do all the talking when we get to the doll hospital."

"All right."

"And no more climbing on chairs and dropping Amelia Jane. I can't afford to keep getting her repaired. Next time it might be you in the hospital for days having your arm and eye mended."

"True. But you have to promise not to hide her anymore and put her on top of the wardrobe. I'll put her away properly."

Nate looked at her. "Deal." He pulled into the parking space at the back of the doll hospital. *I should have done this without her. I really am not looking* forward to this conversation with Miss Monroe. But I can't leave Vianne here on her own.

He got out of the car and let Vianne run in to the red brick building ahead of him. He locked the car and followed slowly.

Susie winked at him from the desk. "She was right. It is a shiner."

Nate's cheeks burned. Had Miss Monroe been boasting over what she'd done? "I'm sorry? Who said what?"

"Vianne. She ran in here, like, saying you'd got a broken nose and a lovely black eye. Was it, like, a run in with a bad guy?"

"Not exactly," Nate said, not having thought he could be any more embarrassed than he already was. "And hello to you too, Miss Vickers."

Susie grinned at him. "Hey, Sgt. Holmes. Dr. A's in the office. I'll, like, give her a shout."

"Thank you." Intrigued as to how that would work, Nate scrutinized Susie as she tapped on the key pad in front of her. Immediately a light flashed on and off several times in the other room.

Susie looked at him though half closed eyes. "Can I, like, sign your plaster?" she teased with teenage enthusiasm.

"Not you, too," Nate groaned. "That's all I had when I went into work this morning."

Susie laughed as Adeline came into reception.

"Sgt. Holmes, do you want to come…" her voice faltered, before she recovered, "…through to the office. Susie, can you take Vianne over to Jasmine to do the discharge paperwork?"

"Sure, Dr. A. Come on, Vianne."

Nate followed Adeline into the office, this time

taking more notice of it. It suited her to a *tee*. A carefree set up that meant she didn't mind what anyone thought. Uncluttered, yet full of knick knacks, it shone with her vibrancy and joy. He shook his head at her offer of coffee and sat down by her desk.

"I'm really sorry about your nose," Adeline said biting her lip. "How is it?"

"Broken."

"Is it very sore?"

Nate held her gaze. "It sticks out like a sore nose." His lips twitched and as a smile spread over her face, he chuckled. "And yes they took the mick out of me something chronic at work when I went in first thing this morning."

"Took the wick?" she asked her face creasing.

"Mick...Mickey... teased me."

"Ah, right." She smiled at him. "Yes, I understand taking the mickey. I just didn't catch what you said. Sometimes if words look similar it's easy to confuse them."

"Ah, right. Anyway as tempting as it was to lie and say a big ten-foot-tall burglar did it..."

Adeline snorted with laughter. "More like a short woman, who shouldn't have been in a tracksuit in the first place."

Nate pushed a hand through his hair. "Why's that?"

"Because someone like me doesn't belong in a self-defense class. Your nose is a prime example. I'm uncoordinated."

"Honestly, you did exactly what I told you to do. In fact you could say I asked for it." He winked. "Literally. So don't feel bad about it, please."

"OK."

"Anyway, as I was saying, as tempting as it was to say it was a ten-foot-tall burglar, I work in M.I.U. so that wouldn't work."

"I'm sorry. I didn't catch that."

"M.I.U." He saw the confused look and wished he could sign it to her. "Murder Investigation Unit."

"Got it." She smiled at him. "What our American friends would call homicide."

Nate nodded. "Yes." His keen gaze took in the pile of newspaper clippings on the corner of her desk. "You're following my case."

Adeline glanced down at them. "Your case?"

"Dane and I are heading this one up. Not that we're making much progress." He drew in a deep breath. "And I didn't just tell you that, either."

"Oh…" She swallowed hard, her bearing changing and becoming distinctly uneasy.

All of Nate's senses kicked into action, his copper's antennae twitching.

She knew something, or at least thought she did.

"What is it?"

Adeline sucked her lower lip into her mouth, worrying it with her teeth. "This is going to sound stupid, but…" She took a deep breath. "I saw them. All of them. They all had their hair tied back or up." She picked up the top clipping. "She was playing on a swing and wearing a red jacket. This one was walking the dog and wearing blue."

Nate jolted as if he'd been struck by lightning. Those details hadn't been released. Was he wrong about her? Was she somehow involved with the murders? "Wait a minute. How did you know any of this?"

Adeline carried on speaking as she sifted through

the papers. "She was on her way to dance class in pink. This one was jogging in a gray toweling track suit and the first one…"

Nate put a hand on her arm, cutting her off.

She jerked her head upwards in surprise.

He held her gaze. "How do you know all this?"

"I told you, I saw them." She took a deep shuddering breath. "Call it a vision or whatever, but, I just see them. Sunday in church, just as we left I lost my balance, and you asked if I was all right."

"I remember. You insisted you were fine, despite my thinking otherwise."

Adeline pulled out the picture. "I saw her on the swing, then on the ground. The same way I saw all the others."

"Do you ever see him?" Nate asked.

"No. I don't think so."

He looked at her. "Let me call Dane. Then I'll take Vianne over to Cassie's, and I'll be back to take a proper statement."

"You believe me?"

Was that surprise on her face? Had she really expected him to laugh at her? Any other cop might have done. Every part of his police training screamed at him to disregard what she'd said and to go with the evidence. But Nate's faith left him open to things that most people wouldn't consider.

"As crazy as it sounds, you just told me things we hadn't released to the press." He stood up. "Let me drop Vianne off and pay you for mending Amelia Jane. She has dozens of dolls, but that one is more important than a teddy bear." He pulled out his wallet and handed Adeline the exact money.

Vianne came running into the office. "Look, she's

all fixed, and she can see now."

Nate smiled at her. "That's wonderful. She looks really good."

Vianne nodded and turned to Adeline. "Thank you for mending her, Dr. Adeline."

"You're welcome. Just take care of her."

"I will." Vianne tugged on her hat. "Much obliged."

Adeline giggled. "I haven't heard that in years. My grandmother's green grocer always used to say that. He had a huge truck filled with fruit and veg. He came around every Saturday afternoon. He'd come to the door and tip his hat just like that and ask if she needed anything. Then he'd go and get it and when Nanna had paid him, he'd say 'much obliged Mrs. Price.'"

Nate grinned. "I think my nan had the same guy. His name was Bill."

"That was him. Dark hair, always wore a green flat cap and had a dark blue jacket on with a blue money bag around his waist." Adeline looked at him. "Wow. Where did your nan live?"

"Onibury Close."

"You're kidding." Her eyes lit up. "Nanna lived at forty-five."

Nate shook his head. *Incredible. So close all these years and never knew.* "Twenty-six. Almost opposite." He smiled. "Anyway, I must go drop Vianne off. I won't be too long."

"Why isn't she in school today?"

"The teachers are on strike. No idea why. They just are." Vianne grinned at Adeline then looked at him. "Have you asked her yet?"

"No."

"Go on, then."

"All right, all right. You're an impatient pumpkin this morning."

"You're the one wanting to leave."

Nate knocked her hat playfully and laughed when she grabbed it and readjusted it. "Miss Monroe, I have something to ask you."

"Please, Sergeant, call me Adeline."

"If you'll call me Nate."

She smiled. "I can do that, Nate."

Shivers ran down his spine and twisted around him. Sudden warmth flooded him at the way his name sounded falling from her lips. For a moment he felt like a giddy school boy and this was before he'd asked her anything. *Get with it. It's not a date. It's just dinner.*

"Then, Adeline, Vianne and I were wondering if…"

Vianne cut him off and grabbed Adeline's hand. "Would you like to come to dinner at our house tonight? Uncle Nate is making wormy mess."

Adeline's eyes widened and her jaw dropped as she looked at Nate. "You're making *what*?"

"Spaghetti bolognaise."

She appeared even more confused and shook her head.

Nate pulled his notebook from his pocket and wrote it down.

"Ah."

"It's not a date," he assured her. "It's just a thank you for fixing the doll and watching Vianne the other day."

"You don't have to."

"I know, and I know you probably don't usually accept dinner from all your patients' relatives, some doctor/patient thing no doubt, but Vianne would like it." *And so would I.* He stood there, his whole body coiled like a spring waiting for her answer.

"He can make other stuff if you don't like worms," Vianne added.

"Spaghetti is good. I'd like to come very much, thank you."

Nate smiled, his heart doing somersaults. And this wasn't a date. However would he react if he ever did ask her out? Where'd that come from? How did I get to this point, Lord? From women aren't to be trusted to considering what it would be like to date her. In less than a week. And after she broke my nose.

"Cool. Then we'll see you about six." He took Vianne's hand. "And Dane and I will be back in a few for that statement."

He led Vianne out to the car and opened the door for her. As she did up her belt, he pulled out his phone. He shut the passenger door as the call connected. "Dane, it's me. We've got a lead on the Herbalist. I'm going to drop Vianne off at the manse and I'll come and get you. But hang on to your hat, because you are not going to believe me when I tell you. No, not over the phone. I'll be with you in ten."

He hung up and hurried around the car. He climbed in and started the engine. "Let's take you over to play with Lara for a bit. I have to work for an hour. Then we can cook dinner."

****

Adeline faced Nate and Dane across her desk. Funny, now she had to repeat her story officially, it sounded even more ridiculous than the first time, and she doubted herself.

Nate pulled out his notebook as Dane laid the paperwork on her desk, to take the statement.

"Just take your time," Nate said. "Tell us everything you remember."

"It's not much," she said. "And it does sound rather farfetched."

"That doesn't matter," Dane told her. "If what Nate said is accurate, you know things that we never released to the press. Any little detail you can give us could be important."

"Don't you guys need physical evidence?"

"Yes, we do. But you volunteered this information, you came to us. Now, however silly your story sounds and however much the Guv laughs at us for taking your statement, that's what we're going to do. Because right now, we need all the help we can get."

"And if it's nothing?"

Nate winked at her. "We arrest you for wasting police time."

Adeline hesitated.

"He's kidding," Dane said quickly. "He's got an appalling sense of humor. Please, tell us what you know."

"All right." As she spoke, she watched the men's hands fly over the paper. Dane's handwriting was large and flowing, whereas Nate's was neat and precise. Both seemed to fit their personalities.

Dane removed his glasses and chewed the arm thoughtfully, before waving them at her. "Did you ever see him?"

"Him? Oh you mean the attacker? It's more of a presence than anything else. Like a shadow. He's there, watching them. It's hard to put into—" Adeline broke off.

She shivered as a sudden chill permeated her whole being from her soul outwards. She closed her eyes, fighting the urge to throw up, as the hauntingly familiar red sheen enveloped her.

"No…" she managed, pushing to her feet. Maybe if she moved, she could outrun the vision this time. Everything faded around her until she was no longer aware of the desk beneath her fingertips.

Long black hair swung in front of her face as she ran, her breath coming in gasps. She tripped and fell. Landing on her hands and knees by the river, blood oozing from the grazes, strong hands turned her over before grasping her neck, squeezing the life from her, his face hidden, as a long, greasy ponytail brushed against her face…

Adeline's hands rose to her throat, trying to pull him away from her. She struggled to breathe, to cry out, to do something, anything. A hand touched her face and her eyelids sprang open. She was lying face up on the floor, her hands outstretched in front of her.

Nate knelt beside her, concern written over his face, his lips moving.

She strained to focus on him, still feeling too choked to speak.

"You're all right. Adeline…"

Tears filled her eyes and spilled down her cheeks. *Please, God, help her. Don't let her suffer.* She signed frantically telling them to go and help the girl before she died, too.

She watched the two men exchange a few words she couldn't catch before Dane left the room rapidly. Too late she remembered neither of them spoke sign language and speech was still beyond her. Perhaps Dane had gone for Jasmine.

Nate's gentle hand turned her face back. "Calm

down. It's all right. You're safe."

She tried to focus on him, but all she could see was the figure on the ground and dark eyes. Black, hollow eyes filled with evil boring into her.

Nate's lips moved, but she couldn't understand what he said. She pulled away from him, signing rapidly. "I don't understand. You have to go and help her, please. He's hurting her."

Dane ran back in with Jasmine, who pulled Adeline into a hug.

Adeline clung to her, huge sobs welling up.

Jasmine's hands moved over her back for a moment, then she pulled away so she could see Adeline's face. "What happened?"

"I don't know." Adeline signed rapidly. The words tumbled from her hands, tears burning her eyes as she relived it. "I saw a girl and a man and he was hurting her. Tell them to stop him before he kills her. Don't let another woman die."

Jasmine's hand covered her mouth and she must have said something because shock and grief covered the two men's faces.

Nate touched her arm and Adeline twisted towards him. He sat on the corner of her desk. He spoke slowly and for once clearly. "I don't understand your signs, Adeline. I need you to speak as well. Did you see something? Another murder? Where?"

"Yes," she signed, letting Jasmine translate for her. "She was by the river. There were swans on the water. She's got long dark hair, is wearing jeans, and an orange strappy top. He chased her, and she fell. There was blood on her knees and hands. He looked as if he was helping her up, but he turned her onto her back, pushing her down. Then he put his hands around her throat…"

Nate and Dane exchanged looks. "Did you see him? A park bench, anything? Something to narrow down the area for us to search."

She shook her head, still only able to sign. "Weeping willow trees, lots of them. Oh, there was a phone tower or pylon or something behind him. He wore a mask, but his eyes…"

"If the time scales the same, we don't have much time. I'll get an all-points bulletin put out along that section of the river. Maybe they'll see someone matching her description." Dane pulled out his phone and turned away to make the call.

Jasmine kept her face towards Adeline as she spoke. "Is she seeing the Herbalist murders, Nate?"

"I wondered that, but the river's nowhere near the—"

Adeline cut him off now calm enough to form words. "He moves the bodies of the girls afterwards. It's not random, where he's leaving them." She reached down and picked Ben up, cuddling him. "I'm all right," she reassured him as he nudged her. She stroked his head and ears, the simple actions calming her.

Jasmine touched her arm. "I want you to go home," she signed as she spoke obviously making it clear there'd be no misunderstanding.

"I'm fine."

Jasmine rolled her eyes and signed rapidly. "Don't make me get Nate and Dane on to you. You're no good to me like this. Go home. Have a bath. Watch some TV. Eat chocolate."

Part of her wanted to argue, to prove she was able to cope, but if she were honest, Adeline knew she couldn't. These visions or whatever drained her. All she wanted to do was go home and pray.

She wouldn't wish this sense of helplessness on anyone. Knowing someone was being hurt and being unable to do anything about it ripped her heart in two. She had no idea why God had given her this 'gift.' Not if it didn't save lives.

Dane came back in. "Nate, we need to roll. Guv wants us to check this out."

Nate nodded. He looked at Adeline and held her gaze. "I'll come pick you up at six."

Confusion filled her for a moment. Why was he picking her up at six? Then she remembered. He was cooking dinner for her. "Won't you be busy now?"

"Vianne is expecting you. I won't let her down. I'll pick you up at six."

"No, it's fine. We'll walk." She held his gaze. "We'll walk," she repeated, signing it as well.

Nate held his hands up in a show of defeat. "All right. You can walk. I'll see you at six. Are you always this stubborn?"

She shrugged slightly. "Mum would say you ain't seen nothing yet. See you at six."

Nate rose and headed to the door.

Dane kissed Jasmine and ran after him.

"Come on Ben. Let's go home." She glanced at Jasmine, knowing she'd never manage the walk home no matter what she'd told Nate. "Can you take me, please? I didn't want to appear weak in front of the men, but these things always take it out of me."

"Sure. Let me lock up and we'll go. And you can fill me in on the way. I want to know how many of 'these things' as you put it you've had and what they mean."

****

Nate got back in the car, slamming the door harder than he needed. He let out a heavy sigh and shoved his hands viciously through his hair. They were too late, again. No sooner had they gotten to the river, than the call came through to go to Clover Drive.

Dane got in and started the car. "Leave the door on the hinges, mate."

"Sorry." Nate took a deep, supposedly calming breath, which did absolutely nothing for his stress levels. "That's six women, Dane. And we still know nothing about him. How many more women are going to die while we faff about doing absolutely nothing?"

Dane twisted in his seat. "All right, first off. We are not messing about. Nor are we doing nothing. We are chasing down every lead we get. Fine, we might not have much to go on, but at least this time there is a witness to talk to, right?"

"Adeline."

"Yes, Adeline. She said there was a connection. That he's moving the girls after he kills them. There must be a reason for that. Perhaps if we talk to her again, we'll be able to work it out."

Nate nodded. "And secondly?" He caught Dane's questioning look. "You said first off. That implies there must be at least a second and possibly a third."

"Secondly, getting mad isn't going to help. What was that verse you quoted at me last week?"

"Philippians chapter four, verses five through seven. *Let your gentleness be evident to all. The Lord is near. Do not be anxious about anything, but in every situation, by prayer and petition, with thanksgiving, present your requests to God. And the peace of God, which transcends all understanding, will guard your hearts and your minds in Christ Jesus."*

"Right." Dane started the car. "Now you, being a church elder, know better than any one that no matter what happens, God is in overall control. He's not sleeping or taking His eyes off the game or dropping the ball."

"Women are dying and there is nothing I can do to prevent it. Except, pray that this time we'll have enough of a lead to catch the creep."

His phone rang and he pulled it out of his pocket. "Holmes. Seriously? Praise God. That's brilliant, we'll go straight there." He looked at Dane. "She's alive. They're taking her to the hospital now."

Dane checked the mirror and did a U-turn. "Good. Maybe we just got another break."

****

Nate leaned against the reception desk in the Emergency Department and shook his head. Frustration filled him to boiling point. *I thought we were getting a break here, Lord. It's not what I see it as. Yes, she's alive, and I thank You for that, but we can't communicate with her. She's deaf. Do I bring Adeline in to talk to her? The Guv won't like it, but it's the best use of resources.*

Dane came back. "The doc says she can talk to us in a bit. But only five minutes. However, unless we get an interpreter in here, five hours won't be enough. She can't speak because of the damage to her throat and vocal chords, and we can't sign."

"Then we use Adeline. Rather than waiting for the hospital or the department to provide an interpreter, we use the assets we have."

"Or we can use Jas. She's well versed in sign, as you saw earlier." Dane's voice conveyed the same level of urgency that filled Nate. "Besides, Adeline is a witness. How do we know she'll give us the victim's version and not the one she saw in her head?"

"This girl is completely deaf. She might find it easier to talk to someone who's also deaf. And yes, I know Adeline saw the attack. It might make her remember something, some little detail that's important."

Nate paused. Why were his feelings here so confused? He didn't have a problem with Adeline being deaf, even when they interviewed her earlier. Was it because she could speak? Or was it something else? A small burgeoning feeling that he had for her? The way his heart leapt when he saw her and defied his every inclination to remain just friends? Or to remain professional. She was a witness in his case. The only witness to a serial murderer. Albeit an unconventional witness.

Shaking his head, he looked at Dane. "Did you check the victim's pockets?"

Dane nodded, holding out the plastic bag. "Clover. Is he trying to tell us something with all these herbs? Maybe it's a recipe for something or other?"

Nate scoffed. "Then he needs to leave instructions with them. Did they find the victim's bag yet?"

"Yeah, down by the river. A uniformed officer is bringing it in. We could get them to pick Adeline up at the same time."

"I'll go," Nate said. Part of him couldn't wait to see her again, while the other doubted his sanity in doing this. "Wait until I get back before you go in."

"Sure."

The nurse came out of the cubicle, and Nate gasped as he saw the figure lying on the bed. Her face badly swollen, and her left hand cut to shreds, she lay looking up at the ceiling.

Dane looked at her. "You know her?"

Nate nodded. "Yeah, I do. She's a friend of Adeline's, and she comes to the self-defense class. Her name's Rachel Stevens." He shook his head and touched his nose ruefully. "Guess I really am a lousy self-defense teacher."

"Why do you say that?"

"One of my pupils breaks my nose and blacks my eye and another ends up half dead."

Dane put a hand on Nate's arm. "You and I both know self-defense only goes so far. She survived. That's what matters. Had it not been for what you taught her, she might not have survived at all. Now go and get Adeline so we can talk to Rachel before they throw us out."

****

Adeline walked close to Nate into the ED, Ben on the leash beside her. Ever since Nate had picked her up, she'd felt sick. Why hadn't she known it was Rachel? Then she realized she hadn't seen the girl's face this time. She'd *been* her, somehow. Seen and experienced the attack from another view point.

Nate held himself stiffly. He was taking this personally.

"It's not your fault, Nate."

"Then whose fault is it?"

Adeline grasped Nate's arm and stood in front of

him. The darkness in his eyes, and the whole aura that surrounded him showed a depth of emotion she'd never seen in a man before. She was filled with an insane urge to hug him. He cared about these women and wanted to put things right before anyone else got hurt. "Nate, you didn't hurt her. The man with the ponytail did."

"Ponytail?" Something flickered in his eyes. "What ponytail? You never mentioned it before."

"I, I'm sorry. I thought I had. I hadn't seen anything of him until this time. His eyes and his hair brushing my, no her face. It was long, dark and greasy and tied back in a ponytail."

"No, you didn't mention it." He turned away for a moment, his posture stiffening yet further until he was as tight as a drum. Was he angry with her for not saying anything? Or was it frustration because he hadn't caught the killer? Then he looked back at her, regaining his composure. "Is there anything else you remember?"

"No."

He jerked his head in response. "I need to interview her, and I need you to translate what she says. We don't have long before the nurse will kick us out to let her rest."

"Sure." Guilt for not telling him immediately about the attacker's ponytail churned her stomach as Adeline plodded after Nate to the cubicle where Rachel lay. He seemed to believe in her visions more than she did. What if this detail wasn't correct, just an image she'd created from some TV drama or an overactive imagination? Despite him calling her a witness, she really hadn't *seen* anything. At least nothing that would stand up in court.

A uniformed officer stood outside the curtain with Dane.

Dane came over to meet them. "For now she'll have a guard, just in case he decides to try again." He smiled at Adeline. "Thanks for coming."

"Welcome." She followed them into the cubicle and looked at Rachel. She stifled a gasp and moved over to the bed. *Why her? She's so badly hurt.*

Ben sat by her feet as Adeline gently touched Rachel's arm, managing a smile as her friend's eyes jerked open. "Hey," she signed. "How are you?"

Rachel's swollen eyes filled with tears. "You shouldn't be here," she signed. "I'm ashamed."

"Don't be. None of this is your fault. You didn't ask him to hurt you."

"I should have fought him off." Rachel's hands moved rapidly. "I should have remembered what Nate showed me. I froze."

Nate tapped Adeline on her arm. "What's she saying?"

Adeline signed as she spoke, so Rachel could follow the conversation. "She feels ashamed. She couldn't do what you taught her and fight him off."

"Tell her she didn't do too badly. She survived."

Adeline signed his words to Rachel and verbalized her response. "I shouldn't have. He didn't want me to survive."

"Can she describe him for us?"

Rachel looked away as Adeline signed. Adeline tapped her arm. "I know it's hard, but you are the only one who's seen him up close, Rachel. They can catch him now; punish him for what he did to you and the others."

Rachel took a deep breath. "Tall," she signed.

"About six foot. Dark eyes. Strong, very strong. His hair was black and tied back—it brushed my face. There was this smell..." She paused, rubbing her throat. "I couldn't breathe."

"What smell?" Adeline asked.

"Garlic. Not just his breath—all of him."

Nate touched Adeline's arm "Ask her if he said anything."

She nodded and turned to Rachel, signing Nate's question.

"I wasn't really paying attention!" Rachel's hands moved irately, her face contorting. "I was too busy dying."

"It's important," Dane said. "Tell her the more we know, the better chance we have of catching him before he does this to someone else."

Adeline repeated it to Rachel and held her gaze. She watched Rachel's response and her eyes widened. She reverted to signing only, wanting to make sure before she said anything to Nate or Dane. "Are you sure, Rach? You didn't read his lips wrong?"

"I know what I saw. I know how easy it is to misinterpret sometimes, but he was so close it was hard to miss." She put a hand in front of her face for a moment. "He was right here. He paused, loosened his grip..." She took a deep breath. "I know what I saw. And he spoke the truth."

"No, he did not."

"Yes, he did. I wish he'd killed me. I deserve nothing less. A perfect world does not need someone like me in it. Please, leave. I need to be alone now." She turned away, tears running down her face.

Adeline turned to the two cops and signed as she spoke. "As he was strangling her, he paused. He leaned down and kissed her cheek. Then he told her she was safe now. No one would harm her ever again. He was protecting her, like all the others."

"Protecting her by killing her?" Nate studied her, confusion filling his blue eyes. "I don't understand. Protecting them from what?"

Adeline's eyes filled with tears, and she looked away.

Nate moved and stood in front of her. "Protecting them from what?" he repeated.

Adeline signed slowly at him, not wanting to verbalize it.

Nate turned to Dane for a moment and then back to Adeline. "I don't understand all this hand waving business," he said, his hands gesticulating in frustration and annoyance. "Just say it out loud and be done with it."

"All the plants are ones with healing properties. This man feels he's healing his victims. He is saving them from themselves and their deformities. There, happy now?" She tugged on Ben's leash and hurried from the cubicle, wanting out of there as soon as possible. Before her emotions got the better of her.

4

Reaching the fresh air of the main road, Adeline sank against the wall, her breath coming in gasps and tears flowing in a never ending stream down her face. Her hands moved over Ben, petting his head.

"Saving them from their deformities? Am I deformed as well, helping to defile a perfect world? I live a normal life. I dance and sing and play the piano and watch TV with the subtitles on. Dane does that so he can hear the TV over the noise of the children playing. I went to a main-stream school and was accepted by almost everyone. This is me. Adeline Monroe, a plump deaf person, who loves ice skating even if I do fall over more than stay upright. And a lot of people think I'm fine the way I am. And Rachel is fine the way she is, too. Different doesn't mean wrong. She's one of God's children, just like me."

Ben licked her hand, and she buried her face in his fur. "Yes, and you think I'm fine as well, you big softy," she told him. He nudged her. Raising her head, she realized that Nate stood beside her. "How much did you hear?"

"I heard enough to know why he's giving you a hug." Nate perched on the wall next to her and handed her a tissue.

"Thanks." Adeline wiped her face and blew her nose.

"This world is far from perfect, you know that. If it

was perfect, then Jesus wouldn't have needed to have been born and died for us."

"I know, but maybe this creep has a point. Rachel's whole life has been a struggle to be accepted, just like mine. And now, when she and I have made it and most people do accept us for what we are, this happens and everything gets turned on its head."

Nate touched her hand. "You are a beautiful woman with a lot to give. Don't ever let anyone tell you any different. And Rachel is, too."

"But our hearing loss…"

"It makes no difference to me or Dane or Jasmine or anyone who really cares about you or Rachel."

"Cares about me?" *Did he just include himself in that sentence or am I reading too much into this?*

"Yes, cares. You have friends and family who do care, a lot. Don't ever believe that you don't. More importantly God cares about you. Remember first Peter chapter five verse seven. *Cast all your cares upon Him, for He careth for you.*"

"That's one of my favorite verses."

"Mine, too." He held her gaze. "Right. Dane's going to finish up here. He and a composite artist are going to get a computer generated description from Rachel and then go home. He's using a text document to talk to her. How about you and I go back to my place and make those messy worms for Vianne?"

A reluctant smile covered her lips. He was still prepared to cook for her, after everything that had happened. "You invite me to dinner and then expect me to help cook it?"

His shoulders shook, and his face lit as he laughed. "Yes, because I'm mean like that and have no idea how to charm and date women properly."

Adeline laughed. Tension left her shoulders. It was nice to know there was still humor in the world, especially at a time like this. "Then it's a good job this isn't a date."

"It certainly is. And yes, I meant what I said about being friends. Come on. I even have something Ben can eat."

Ben's ears pricked up and Adeline smiled. "Thank you. But don't you and Dane want to discuss the case, follow leads and so on?"

"There's nothing more I can do tonight, but it will be full on in the morning. Maybe we could talk after dinner, once Vianne is in bed. I'd like to know a little more about you. But if you'd rather help me figure things out, then that would be good, as well."

"Sure, we can do both."

Nate stood and offered a hand.

Burning heat shot through her hand as he hauled her upright.

"Then let's go. Messy worms await."

****

Adeline sat on the bar stool in the kitchen.

Nate sure knew his way around the stove, and the meat sauce smelled heavenly.

Thank you for bringing him into my life the way You did. Even if all we ever are is friends, then my life is blessed for that.

Nate glanced at her. "What are you thinking? You have this enigmatic smile on your face."

"Just thinking how domesticated you look in your apron. The human side of the police force."

Nate smiled. "I try. Honestly, I never cooked much

before Vianne. But you can only give a child so much junk food and frozen TV dinners. She bought me the apron a couple of Christmas's ago when I managed to spill tomato puree down a white shirt and couldn't get the stains out."

A small hand tapped her foot and Adeline glanced down.

"Junk food is bad for you," Vianne said, fondling Ben's ears absently. "Too many chips make you fat. And give you heart disease"

"Do they?"

Vianne nodded. "So do burgers. We're learning about it at school. I like what Uncle Nate makes. He calls them proper dinners." She tilted her head. "Do you like toad in the hole?"

Adeline nodded. "I make that a lot. It's my favorite. I like cauliflower cheese, too. And roast beef."

"I love that. We don't have it often enough. Uncle Nate works too much to do a roast. He says they take too long to make and I'd be in bed by the time it was ready."

"Then how about on Sunday you and Uncle Nate come to my house after church for lunch. We'll have roast beef, then."

Vianne turned to Nate. The angle of her head precluded Adeline from reading her lips, but Nate's response was all too clear.

"She's a witness. I can't..." He broke off as Vianne gesticulated wildly. "I know, but this is—"

Adeline looked away not wanting to see his excuses. So much for the two of them being friends. She had finally met a bloke who treated her like a 'normal' person and now this. It wasn't fair. She looked back at him. "I can go if you'd rather not be seen consorting with a witness."

Nate shook his head. "This is different."

She frowned, really not seeing how, but not going to ask. She felt uncomfortable enough now as it was. "It's no different at all. But, if you don't want to come or you can't because of work, I don't have a problem with that. But perhaps Vianne could come to my place for dinner after school one night. I'll feed her, and you can pick her up when you finish your shift."

Vianne shot her a beaming smile. "That would be wonderful. Please, Uncle Nate?"

"All right." He scrutinized Adeline, and she shivered under the intensity of his gaze. Her heart pounded, threatening to jump into her throat and suffocate her. How could he be so nice one minute and then cold the next? Was he so used to playing good cop-bad cop that he did it off duty, as well?

"Cool." Vianne's smile lit her entire face.

Nate turned his gaze to his niece. "Now go wash your hands while I dish up."

"Yes, Uncle Nate." She scrambled to her feet and ran from the room.

"Nate..." Adeline spoke hesitantly. "If you'd rather she didn't come to dinner until this case is over, I don't mind. I don't want to do anything to jeopardize things at work for you."

"It's fine. How about Wednesday? I don't finish until seven, then."

She nodded. "Wednesday's good."

A smile finally crossed Nate's face, although it never reached his eyes. "Thank you."

"Welcome."

Nate brought the plates over just as Vianne ran back into the room. She had yet another hat pulled down over her hair. What was with the child and hats?

Just as Nate sat down, he rolled his eyes and pulled his phone from his pocket. "I have to take this. Please, start eating, I won't be long. Vianne, say grace." He pushed his chair back and left the table. "Holmes."

Adeline nodded, her eyes following him from the room. Worry had settled on his face and he didn't say more than his name before he left the room. Adeline wondered. Was it Rachel? Had something more happened to her? Or worse, had the Herbalist struck again?

Vianne touched her hand. "I'll say grace." She closed her eyes. "Thank You, God, for this nice dinner. Amen."

"Amen." Adeline picked up her fork.

Vianne stabbed her spaghetti with a fork. "This happens a lot. He works way too much."

"He's got a very important job."

"I can think of a more important one."

Adeline took a mouthful. The food was as delicious as it both looked and smelled. "What's that?"

"He needs a wife. He shouldn't be alone the way he is."

Adeline choked on her spaghetti. She reached for the glass of water. "Really?"

"God doesn't want him to be alone. It says so in the Bible. And if I had an auntie, then I wouldn't be palmed off on babysitters so much. Assuming she was a stay-at-home auntie and not a works-all-the-hours-God-gives-her auntie."

Adeline took several swallows of the water, wondering how to respond.

She knew marriage was the preferred state, and God designed men and women for that. However, it was also true that He called some people to remain single, that they might serve Him better that way. It was hard. She knew all too well how hard it was to be alone. She prayed daily for the one special person she hoped was waiting for her. But she also knew that God constantly gave her the strength to face every day alone.

Looking at Vianne, Adeline smiled. "Uncle Nate told you that, did he?"

"No. Uncle Dane told him one night when I was playing in the hall. I have a list of candidates. Would you like to see it?"

"Maybe when you come to dinner on Wednesday. I don't think you want Uncle Nate overhearing your list."

Vianne's choice of language was impressive, if a little adult at times. She obviously spent way too much time with adults rather than children her own age.

"Did you want to apply? I can add your name after dinner."

"Me?" Adeline choked again, this time sparking a proper coughing fit. Her eyes watered and she was dimly aware of someone thumping her back. Finally, the lump shifted and she could breathe.

Nate stood there, holding out fresh water.

She took it and swallowed several large mouthfuls. "Sorry."

"Are you all right?"

She nodded. "It just went down the wrong way."

"Vianne said it had bones in it."

"No. It's really nice."

Nate sat down. "So long as you're all right."

"I'm fine." Adeline glanced at Vianne, who put a finger to her lips. She nodded and picked up her fork again.

****

After dinner, with Vianne taking her time in the bath, Nate smiled across at Adeline. He'd been wrong earlier in the way he'd spoken to her. But she'd accepted his apology, which was good. And despite choking on the food, she appeared to have enjoyed it and so far escaped without any repercussions.

"You realize I've never cooked for a woman before," he told her.

"Really? Doesn't Vianne count?" She sipped her coffee, the other hand petting Ben.

"You know what I mean. Since Pete died, I haven't had time to do anything other than be a surrogate father. I always saw myself as married with kids by now. Guess I have the kids, well kid, but it's not the same."

"Do you wish things were different?"

"Sometimes. It'd be nice to come home to another adult to talk to, to have dinner ready occasionally."

"Just occasionally?"

"Well, maybe seven nights a week…" He wasn't sure his teasing tone carried over in lip reading so he winked at her to prove his point.

Adeline laughed. "Would she have to have your pipe filled and your slippers by the fire?"

"Naturally, though I'd have to start smoking first." He sipped his coffee. "The house would be spotless, and she'd change from her work dress and apron into an evening gown, and wait on me hand and foot."

"You know she doesn't exist except in your mind, right?"

Nate snorted. "Yeah, but a man can dream, can't he?"

"As long as he knows the difference between the dream and reality." Adeline grinned.

"I do."

"Just as well, because the perfect woman isn't me and I'm pretty sure I'm never likely to be."

Nate eyed her. "That's fine with me. Perfection is over rated. I like women who know their own mind and work at jobs they love, whether it's at home or somewhere else. I like women who enjoy life, good food, and aren't so into their looks it becomes an obsession. Like you. You look nice."

Color flooded her cheeks. "You're just saying that."

"No, I mean it." He smiled at her. "You look great in whatever you wear. Not everyone can do that, but you can. There is nothing wrong with the way you look. Or dress. Or do your hair. Don't let anyone ever tell you otherwise. And that includes yourself."

"Thank you."

"Welcome." He grimaced at the sound of splashing from above. "I'm convinced she'll bring the ceiling down one day when she splashes so much. It sounds like she's bath skating again."

"Bath skating?" Confusion clouded Adeline's face.

He smiled. "It's where you sit on the top of the angled part of the bath at the back and slide down into it. Water goes everywhere." He demonstrated with his hands, parodying the kid's song from Sunday School. "Kind of Vianne came down and the floods went whoosh."

Adeline's laugh echoed like silver bells. "Does she wear a hat in the bath, too?"

"And in bed. She is never without one. She'll wash and dry her hair and put the hat back on before coming downstairs."

"What about school?"

"A hat is part of the uniform, so they tolerate it in class."

Adeline put the cup down and held his gaze. "If you don't mind me asking, what is it about the hats?"

Nate studied his hands for a long moment, wondering how to explain something he didn't fully understand himself. "Most kids, from what I've been told, have a security blanket. Usually it's a teddy, a comforter, blanket, dummy or something similar, which they take everywhere at first. To start with, Vianne didn't have anything like that. No special toy or anything. Pete joked she was the only child in the history of the world who didn't need one special thing to help her sleep."

"I had a bear. It had fifteen names."

"I had a rabbit, but don't tell anyone that." The memories of those first few difficult months with Vianne were painful even after all these years. "After Pete and Ophelié died, Vianne became very withdrawn and clingy for several weeks. She wouldn't leave my side, not even for Sunday School, with me in the main church building. She would doze on the sofa until I went to bed, and then insisted on sleeping on the floor next to my bed, or I'd have to camp out in the room she'd chosen for herself. So, one Sunday, I wore my baseball cap to church and when we got there, I gave it to her to wear. Told her that way she knew I'd come and collect her after Sunday School because she had my hat."

"I guess it worked."

Nate grinned. "I didn't get the hat back. In fact, she wore it everywhere. It took six months, and a lot of hard work, before I could buy her a hat of her own. I assume she feels safe when she wears one. Equates it with knowing someone is always coming to get her."

"It's good she has that. And you. You do a wonderful job of caring for her."

"I try. It's my intention that I'll always be there for her." He put his coffee down and held out his arms as Vianne came running into the room. "There you are, pumpkin. You all ready for bed, now?"

She ran into his arms and hugged him tightly. "Yes, and I've cleaned my teeth. I'm ready for my story and prayers now."

"Good girl." He got to his feet. "I'll be back in a few, once I've put Vianne to bed."

"I'll be here." Adeline smiled.

****

Vianne went to bed easier than Nate anticipated, but he wasn't going to complain.

Having gone up expecting a fight, he was pleasantly surprised not to get one. That was a relief. He needed to tell Adeline about the phone call and what Dane had found out. He went back downstairs, to find Adeline flicking through the photo album from the table.

Ben tapped her on the arm and she looked up and smiled. "These pictures are good. Did you take them?"

Nate nodded, sitting next to her. "I did and thank you."

"You should sell some of them. This one is wonderful." She pointed to a sunset over the lake. Two swans sat in the foreground, their beaks touching, an orange glow surrounding them and the water rippling beside their bodies.

He cringed with embarrassment. "I just happened to be there. Anyone could have taken it."

"Not everyone would have captured the essence of the moment. You have a talent."

Heat rose in his cheeks. No one had praised his work in a long time. "Thank you."

Adeline flicked a few more pages. "Wow, look at all those bluebells. Where's this?"

"Christmas Common. Vianne loves the bluebells, we go every year. I have an album just with her and the flowers." He took a deep breath, not wanting to spoil the moment, but needing to broach the subject of the phone call.

Putting a hand on the book, he closed it gently. "Adeline, I need to talk to you."

"You look serious. What's up?"

"The phone call during dinner was Dane. We've got, well not a lead exactly, but a connection between all the victims."

"Should you be telling me this? After all I'm one of your witnesses, remember."

"I know you're officially a witness, and I discussed the point with Dane. Fact is, we both agree you need to know. So you can take precautions."

Adeline caught her breath. "What kind of precautions? Are you saying the Herbalist knows who I am?"

"Nothing like that. I just want you to be extra vigilant, that's all." He took a deep breath, looking at her intently. He made sure he spoke carefully, not wanting her to misinterpret any of his words. "We just had it confirmed that the Herbalist is only targeting disabled people. Deaf, lame, short-sighted and so on. In fact anything that deviates from the norm."

He could almost see the bristles rising as Adeline straightened. Ben leapt off her lap and stood guard next to her. He wasn't sure if he imagined the bared teeth or whether Ben actually did it momentarily.

Indignation colored her voice, and fire shot from her eyes. "Are you saying I'm disabled?"

Nate backtracked, annoyed with himself, trying to think of a better word. "No, I'm not saying that at all."

"Then what are you saying, Sergeant?" Her use of his title indicated he'd crossed a line.

"You know what I mean."

Anger creased her face, spilling over into her hand gestures and voice. "No, I don't. I'm not disabled or disadvantaged. I'm deaf. You said earlier it didn't matter, or was that a lie? Something you tell all your witnesses just to keep them happy? Something to calm them down, stop them crying."

"Disabled was the wrong word, I accept that."

"Would you prefer deformed or crippled or maimed?"

Nate turned away.

Her anger was blistering, but fully justified.

Lord, help me find a way to calm her, explain properly.

"Don't you do that. You know I can't hear you if you turn your face away." Adeline moved and stood in front of him. Her eyes glittered, and she rapidly signed at him, not saying a word. He knew from the vehemence of her movements that she was angry, no, way more than angry, she was furious with him.

Nate didn't understand any of what she was

trying to tell him. She may as well have been speaking Portuguese or Russian for all the difference it made. Frustrated at the communication gap, he reached out and grabbed her hands. As he did so, something almost electrical passed between them. He looked at her, holding her gaze, and moved closer to her. Before he realized what he was doing, he leaned in, and his lips brushed against hers.

Her mouth was soft under his and her body molded against him as if they were made for each other. He looked at her, but she had her eyes closed.

He slid a hand into her hair, and placed the other on small of her back, holding her close as he kissed her.

****

Adeline parted her lips slightly, giving him control as he deepened the kiss. Her arms slid around Nate's neck and she leaned against his firm body. Her eyes closed, leaving her fully immersed in his touch and taste. She could taste the coffee and a hint of the herbs from dinner. Ripples of pleasure ran through her, radiating outwards until all that mattered was Nate and the feelings he sent spiraling through her.

The simple touch warmed her completely, lighting a fire within she wasn't sure would ever go out. All she knew was that she didn't want it to. She kissed him back, eager to take what he offered, to give back as much as she took.

The kiss went on forever, until just as she thought she'd never breathe again, he pulled away. Adeline opened her eyes. His hands slid to her shoulders, her skin burning under his touch. Adeline held his gaze, still able to feel him on her lips. "Do you kiss everyone you argue with?"

"Not usually." He held her gaze as he ran a finger slowly over her swollen lips. "You didn't seem to object."

"I've never been kissed before."

"Seriously? I'd never have known."

She held his gaze, not daring to hope he meant anything by the kiss "Never...being 'disabled' tends to scare men off."

"I'm sorry I said that. It was unforgivable. I feel horrible."

"So you should. But I'll forgive you if you promise not to do it again."

"I promise." Nate hugged her, and she leaned against him, marveling at the warmth a simple hug could give. She could stay in his arms forever, if only it were possible.

After a long moment she pulled back to smile at him.

Nate smiled back. "You're amazing."

"I don't think so. I've never been called that before. I've been called lots of other things, but not that."

His fingers caressed her face. "Well, I think so."

Adeline closed her eyes and leaned into his touch, one hand pressed against the firmness of his chest, the other resting on his throat. She could feel his heart beating under her fingers, the rise and fall of his breathing. Standing there she felt safe and...she hesitated to say loved. She knew she cared for him. Cared very much what happened to him and about him, but was it love or was it just the emotions of the moment making her head spin.

Vibration under her fingers made her open her

eyes. She focused on his lips just as they finished moving.

"…care."

"I didn't catch that, I'm sorry."

"No problem. I said, you need to take care out there."

"Why? And don't give me any more of that disabled rubbish. Ben takes wonderful care of me, and I've been doing this since I was five."

"I don't want anything happening to my niece's favorite dolly doctor."

A sinking feeling settled in her stomach. She *was* reading too much into this after all. She looked down. "I see."

Gentle fingers lifted her face. A smile teased the corner of his lips, lighting his eyes. They shone with an inner beauty she hadn't noticed before. "But more because I care about what happens to you."

"I care about you, too."

He smiled properly. "I'm glad."

She glanced at the clock above the mantelpiece. "It's getting late. I should go."

"Let me call you a cab."

"No, I can walk. Ben needs a walk before bed, anyway."

"Then I insist you call me as soon as you get home. I won't sleep tonight unless I know you're safe."

"I will. I promise."

"Good. Stay here and I'll get your coat."

Adeline slid into her coat. "Thank you for dinner. Are you sure you won't join us on Wednesday? Or am I still just a witness?"

"You're more than just a witness," Nate said. "But I still won't finish before seven."

"That's fine. Vianne can have a snack after school, and we'll eat with you."

"I'd like that very much."

"Then it's a date." Adeline paused, as the realization of what she said sunk in.

"Just dinner is fine. And don't forget to call when you get in." He made no reference to her slip.

"I won't." She headed down the road; her heart in her boots by Ben's trotting paws. She was a fool.

5

Wednesday came quickly, and having buried herself in fixing broken toys all day long, Adeline finished work as soon as Vianne arrived after school. She was glad of the change of pace.

Perhaps this would call a halt to the images running through her mind's eye ever since she jerked awake at three AM with a nightmare. "Hey, ready to go?"

Vianne looked at her. "Now? Can't I visit with some of the dolls first?"

"We need to get home and put the meat in the oven." Adeline clipped on Ben's lead. She straightened to find Vianne scowling at her. "What's that face for?"

"I want to read to the dollies." Vianne stamped her foot for added emphasis.

"I want, doesn't get."

"That's what Uncle Nate says all the time." She folded her arms across her chest, bottom lip sticking out.

"Then it must be true." Adeline looked at the frowning child. This wasn't a great start. If she didn't leave now, the meat would either be as tough as old boots or not cooked at all. "Do you know how to make Yorkshire puddings?"

"No."

"Want to learn?"

Vianne's face brightened. "Really? I'm not allowed

to cook at home. It's 'too dangerous.'" She put quote marks around the last two words, rolling her eyes as she spoke.

"Especially the way I do it." Adeline laughed. "I'll teach you, and we won't tell him 'til after he's eaten."

"Cool." Vianne beamed at her. "So what are we waiting for?"

****

By the time Ben told Adeline there was someone at the door at seven fifteen, the kitchen no longer resembled the bomb site it had been all afternoon. The flour had been cleared off the surfaces and floor, batter wiped from the cupboard doors and Vianne's face. She even picked the remnants of the egg shell from the sugar bowl.

She opened the door and let Nate in out of the rain. "Hey."

"Hey. Something smells good." Nate entered the house, shedding his wet coat.

"Thank you." She took the coat and hung it on the free standing coat rack set in one corner of the hallway. "This is soaked."

Nate nodded. "I was outside all afternoon at a crime scene. Uniformed officers got the call this morning, and we spent the afternoon talking to the neighbors in the hope of finding something useful."

Adeline held his gaze. Sorrow filled his eyes again, this time seeming to permeate to his soul. She should have called him, but one thing after another had come up and... "The Herbalist?"

"Yeah. He made sure this one died. She was only fifteen." He took a deep breath, raw emotion crossing his face. "It doesn't matter how many of these I do, I never become immune to it."

"Was there an herb cutting in one of her pockets?"

Nate's eyes narrowed. "Yes, there was. How did you—?"

"And it matches the name of the road." She closed her eyes, and then stared unwavering at him. "Toadflax."

Nate took a deep breath, and suddenly looked beyond her. His face changed in an instant from a concerned frown into a broad smile. "Hey, pumpkin. How was your day?" He moved past her and swung Vianne into his arms.

Adeline moved into the kitchen to check on the food. He was right. This conversation was not one to be had in front of a child. She glanced down at Ben. "I know what you're thinking, but I'm not running to him every time I have a nightmare or one of those vision things. He's the detective. He can put the pieces together all by himself without my rubbish interpretation. And don't tell me that makes me accountable. Or guilty by association."

Ben cocked his head at her and put a paw over his nose. Adeline screwed her nose up at him. "Ack, get over it. I've put one and one together and made five."

He knocked her foot and looked behind her.

Her stomach dropped into her slippers as she saw Nate standing there. Heat rushed to her cheeks, and she hoped he'd assume it was heat from the stove causing the blush and nothing more.

****

"What makes five?" Nate asked, as he followed

Vianne into the kitchen.

"Two plus three, silly," Vianne giggled as she sat at the table.

Adeline was covering something, but the question was what? Had she known about the latest murder and not told him?

"Five thousand. We've made enough to feed the five thousand, so I hope you're hungry."

"We?"

"Vianne stirred the gravy and crumbled in the Oxo cubes. That's the most important job."

"I also made the Yorkshire puddings," Vianne added, bouncing on her chair. "Or I helped to. I wasn't allowed to put them in the hot fat, but I beat the mixture."

Nate's stomach growled and he was grateful Adeline couldn't hear it. Breakfast was hours ago, and he'd worked through lunch. Rather, lunch still sat on his desk, a paltry two bites taken from the sausage roll he'd bought from the canteen. "Can I do anything?"

"No, just sit down and wait patiently. It won't be long."

Nate perched on a chair by the table, watching Adeline as she moved around the kitchen, half listening to Vianne rabbiting on about her day at school. The other part of his mind, the cop part that never switched off, went over and over Adeline's words. There was only one way she could know about the herbs left on the victims. Unless she knew the killer, and he doubted that.

Adeline brought over the first dishes, her eyes clouded with sorrow, as she took in the plaster still adorning his face. "How's your nose?"

"Sore, but a lot less painful than it has been. I

should be able to lose this plaster thing soon, hopefully."

"Your eyes look better. Have you considered make-up to hide the bruises?"

Nate looked aghast at her. "I'm a bloke. Blokes do *not* wear make-up."

"Sure they do. Actors and news readers do it all the time. I can show you how to use just a little foundation to hide it."

"It's fine. Thank you all the same."

Vianne tugged Adeline's arm to get her attention. "He thinks it's manly to have bruises," she said. "Improves his street cred, or so Uncle Dane says, and makes the bad guys a-feared of him when he's playing bad cop."

Adeline laughed.

Nate frowned. "When you two have quite finished teasing me…"

Vianne hugged him. "We have."

He wiggled her nose and then tickled her, making her squeal with laughter. "And I'll have you know that I'm the good cop. Uncle Dane is the bad cop."

"Uh huh," she squealed, trying to get away.

Nate let her go. "Yes, uh huh, he is."

"Dinner's ready." Adeline turned to Vianne. "Run upstairs, and wash your hands."

Vianne nodded and ran from the room. Nate moved over to Adeline and touched her arm. He held her gaze, needing to get her to open up to him. It worked with the criminals if he did it long enough. As did the silent treatment—although good cop-bad cop in tandem with Dane was far more effective.

"I should dish up."

"I know. First I need to know something. How did

you know the Herbalist puts herbs in the victim's pockets?"

"I just do."

He tightened his grip a little as she tried to pull away. "It's important, Adeline. No one knows that except Dane, the Guv, me, and the coroner. It's not even in the files in case it gets leaked to the press."

"I saw it," she said finally looking him in the eye. "Last night. I dreamed the whole thing. Saw him stalk her and kill her. He put the herbs in her pocket. They were in a small clear plastic bag. One of those self-sealing ones."

"Then why didn't you tell me?" Nate's voice rose automatically, anger and frustration filling him. "You have my number, you could have called me. You *should* have called me."

Adeline signed jerkily as she spoke. "I'm sure you'd love me ringing you every time I have a nightmare. Especially at three in the morning."

"If it's a dream that concerns the Herbalist, then yes, I do want you ringing me, no matter what time of night it is. We might have gotten to her in time."

Adeline shook her head, her eyes glistening. "She didn't stand a chance. No one does. And you know something? She didn't have one of your 'disabilities' like all the others did. He didn't kill her because she was deaf or short sighted or—"

Nate narrowed his eyes, his stomach twisting at her use of the word. "Then why?"

"Ask him when you catch him."

"I'm asking you. You can't just drop something like that on me and leave it at that."

Adeline turned her face away.

Nate waited impatiently. He could just turn her

face back towards him, but it would be better for both of them if he didn't. He tapped his foot, desperate for the information. It seemed an eternity before she turned back to face him. "Well? How was she different?"

Adeline's voice trembled as she spoke. He'd wondered if she was capable of raw emotion in her voice, and she was. "You need to interview her father. The herbalist was saving her from him."

****

Approaching Nate's house two days later, Adeline consulted Ben. "Are we doing the right thing? Just dropping around unannounced like this? What if they're out?"

Ben regarded her with deep, soulful eyes. He must be the epitome of puppy dog eyes because she could never resist him.

"I know, post it through the door. Maybe that would be better. I mean, we didn't exactly part on good terms the other night. Dinner was decidedly frosty after the dream incident."

Adeline raised a hand to ring the doorbell and hesitated. Maybe she should just shove it through the door. She lowered her hand, intending to get a pen from her bag, so she could write on the package, when the door opened.

Nate stood there with an empty milk bottle in his hand. "Oh, Adeline…hi."

"Hi, I was passing and thought I'd call in on the off chance you were in."

The stiffness in his body as he set the milk bottle on the step, gave away the unease he felt. He straightened and then replied. "We're in. How are you?"

"Fine. You?"

"Yeah. Fine. So's Vianne."

"Speaking of Vianne, I have something for her. Is she around?"

"She's watching TV. Come in for a few."

"Thank you." She guessed he shouted for Vianne because she appeared in the hallway. "Hi, Vianne."

"Hi. How are you?" Vianne carefully signed as she spoke.

"I'm good. How are you?"

Vianne revealed a gap toothed smile. "Good," she signed. Then she went back to speaking. "Did I get it right?"

"You did."

"Yay. And the tooth fairy is coming later. At least I hope she is. Jodie got a pound when her tooth fell out. But Uncle Nate says it depends on whether the tooth fairy has been paid or not as to how much she leaves."

"Sounds about right. I have something for you." Adeline signed carefully. She held out the bag she was carrying to Vianne.

"What is it?"

"Open it and see."

Vianne tore into the bag and a huge grin split her face and filled her eyes. "Cool." She pulled out the baseball cap. "Thank you." She flung her arms around Adeline and hugged her.

Adeline hugged her back. "You're welcome."

After a minute, Vianne pulled away and very hastily replaced her hat with the new one.

Adeline got a very swift glimpse of short auburn curls before they vanished under the new hat. "Very nice."

Vianne smiled and dropped into sign. "Thank you. Do I look pretty?" She twirled around.

"You look lovely." Adeline signed back. She glanced at Nate seeing a smile on his face, but something else in his eyes. "What is it?"

"Just feeling a little left out here. Could you teach me sign language?"

She raised an eyebrow. "Is that so you can interrogate the victims by yourself?"

Nate blushed and looked down and then away.

Adeline sighed and moved to stand in front of him. She signed rapidly, not saying a thing.

A wry smile crossed Nate's face. "I guess I deserved that. No, I want to learn sign so that I can communicate with you."

Adeline moved her hands slowly as she spoke. "Yes, I'd love to teach you."

"Maybe I could start by learning how to say 'I'm sorry'. It's something I seem to say an awful lot."

"That's as good place as any." Adeline showed him and smiled as he repeated it correctly.

****

Two days later, Susie hadn't arrived at work or called in.

Adeline sat on the desk, phone in hand. She'd tried calling several times, but there was no answer. She was more than slightly irritated now and had several versions of the conversation she needed to have with her errant receptionist running through her mind. She hung up for the tenth time when the light over the door flashed and Ben nudged her leg.

Glancing from Ben to the door, she smiled as the customer walked in.

His bleached blond hair, pulled back into a tight ponytail needed re-dying as the roots were showing. His ice cold, blue eyes glittered as they raked over her. A broken doll dangled carelessly from his left hand.

Adeline shivered. Something about him set every nerve on edge and made her skin crawl. Managing a smile anyway, she looked directly at him. "Can I help you?"

"I need the doll fixed. Now, if possible. She won't sleep without it."

"Sure." Adeline took the doll and looked it over. She glanced at the customer. He seemed agitated, if his pacing was any indication. He moved over to the door and looked through the window.

She turned her attention back to the doll. It'd be a simple job, one he probably could have done himself if he'd thought about it. But if he was willing to pay her, then she wasn't going to complain. "It'll take five minutes."

The man glanced at her. "That's fine. How much do I owe you?"

"Three fifty." Adeline didn't need a calculator or the till to work it out. She swiftly fixed the doll. Every time she glanced up the bloke was either pacing or watching out of the window. A couple of times she found his eyes raking over her. She worked faster, eager to get him out of her shop as soon as possible.

Ben stood by her legs, his hackles raised.

She was grateful Jasmine was working in the back. One shout and she would come running.

"There you go. All fixed." She held out the doll.

The man pulled a crisp new ten pound note from

his wallet and handed it over. "Keep the change." He took the doll, his cold and clammy fingers brushing against hers, and left.

Rivers of ice surged though her veins as he touched her. She shuddered and lost her balance. Something dark permeated his soul. She closed her eyes tight as the door shut. Something bad was going to happen. But unlike before, all she had was a feeling. Was disaster going to befall the man who touched her? Was that it? Would he be hit by a car or cause an accident? Whatever it was, death walked with him.

She took a deep breath. Yea, though I walk through the valley of the shadow of death, I will fear no evil: for Thou art with me; Thy rod and Thy staff they comfort me.

Adeline expelled a deep breath and looked down at Ben. "Not even a thank you. Oh well, at least he left a tip." Ben covered his nose with his paw and Adeline laughed. "My sentiments exactly."

Her thoughts took a different turn. Ponytail—was it him? Or was she just being ridiculous now? She'd never seen his face, just his eyes and a glimpse of his hair. If only she'd heard his voice, then maybe…

Adeline closed her eyes trying to visualize the man from her nightmares. Ben nudged her foot, and she opened them to see Jasmine standing at her elbow. She pulled her mind off the stranger and onto work. "Did you manage to get that teddy stitched up all right?"

Jasmine nodded. "I sure did. Do you have any idea what Vianne did to him to cause a rip like that?"

"Nate washed it in the machine. He killed it—according to Vianne."

"Oh dear. Is that another case of child abuse?"

"In capital letters, no less. She wanted to put

murder down, but I talked her out of that one. We settled for intent to cause grievous bodily harm."

Jasmine chuckled. "You can tell she's a cop's niece. She knows way too much. Did he peg it to the line by its ears, too?"

Adeline's smile widened. "Yep."

"Oh boy. She must really hate him this time. Jodie didn't talk to me for a couple of hours when I did that to her stuffed elephant."

"Vianne'll get over it. She always does." She paused. "Did you see that guy that was in here just now? Blond hair, ponytail."

Jasmine shook her head. "No. Why? Did he run off without paying or something?"

"Far from it, he overpaid and told me to keep the change. But there was something about him. His eyes…" She broke off. She'd seen those eyes before. "It was him."

"Who him?" Jasmine signed as she spoke.

"The man from my nightmares. He changed his hair color and wore those odd-colored contact lenses to change his appearance."

Jasmine crossed her arms. "Call Nate. Now. He believes in your visions and so on. It could be nothing. Then again…"

Adeline reached for the phone and dialed Nate. She shook her head. "It's engaged."

Rather than leave a voice mail, she sent him a text. *'Nate, call me, it's urgent.'*

Jasmine shook her head. "He and Dane are on duty. Probably out on the streets somewhere. If he doesn't answer, it means he's in the middle of something really important. He'll get back to you. Tell you what you need? A change of scene. Listen, the

Prime Minister's due to dedicate the new memorial garden in about twenty minutes. Why don't you go and watch?"

Not really wanting to go out on the streets, Adeline signed a response. "I have a lot to do. I can't take time off to go and see someone I can see on the television every day. And it's not as if I voted for her party, either. I voted the same way I always do."

"For the party that doesn't stand a chance of winning."

"Exactly. All the more reason I can't go."

"Course you can go. Look, Ben needs a walk, right? So go for a walk towards the memorial garden. If you happen to see the Prime Minister, all well and good. If not..." Jasmine shrugged. "You had a break. Maybe you can catch Nate, or he'll return your call. You might be able to speak to him for a few minutes."

"Nate won't be there. They'd have all the uniformed officers out, not the murder squad."

Adeline took a deep breath. Perhaps she was imagining things after all and the fresh air would do her good. And with Ben and the Lord with her, what more did she need? "Oh, why not?" She ruffled Ben's ears. "Fancy going to see the Prime Minister?" He cocked his head at her. "Go for a walk?"

He ran off, coming back in a few seconds with his lead hanging from his mouth.

She shook her head. "I guess we're going out. Although I think the magic word there was walk, not go see the Prime Minister."

Jasmine smiled. "I'll try to reach Susie again while you're gone."

"Thank you. If need be I'll swing by her place on my way home tonight to make sure she's all right. Tell you this much. If she is skiving, she's gonna be in trouble." Adeline slid into her jacket. "Come on, Ben." He moved over to her. She clipped on the lead and headed outside.

Warm sunshine streamed through the trees, leaving dappled shadows on the ground by her feet. A pleasant change from the drizzle they'd had all morning. The closer she got to the memorial garden, the more security seemed to outnumber the spectators.

It looks like a police convention. I might not see a thing.

She made her way to the edge of the crowd, finding a space right on the corner of the street to stand. Pulling her phone from her pocket, Adeline started taking photos to show Jasmine. It wasn't every day a famous person visited her part of England.

Glancing across the street, she saw the man again. He was standing on the corner, leaning by a lamppost, a camera in one hand and the doll hanging from the other. He looked totally bored and thinking quickly, she took his photo, too.

If it was him she had a photo to show Nate. If not, she'd delete it. As she watched, the man moved away and into one of the buildings behind him.

Nate raised a hand from where he stood on the opposite side of the road. Adeline waved back. What was he doing here? She slowly signed to him. "I need to speak to you."

Nate frowned. "What?"

She wouldn't have heard him over the crowded street anyway, but reading lips made it easy.

He turned to Dane and spoke rapidly. Dane nodded, and Nate started towards her.

Her breath caught as the Prime Minister's car stopped almost in front her. Somewhat awestruck, she brought her phone up, taking several shots as Prime Minister Williams got out of the car and smoothed down her suit. Adeline had never been this close to anyone famous before and felt ridiculously nervous. It wasn't as if she was going to meet Prime Minister Williams, was it?

Nate edged closer, waving his ID at the security men.

Then Prime Minister Williams was in front of her, with an outstretched hand, and a smile on her lips that never quite made it to her eyes. "Hello, how are you?"

Completely overwhelmed, Adeline reached out and shook her hand. "Hello. I'm fine, how are you?"

"I'm fine, thank you."

Ben held out a paw and the Prime Minister leaned over shaking it. "What a lovely dog."

"Thank you. He's a service dog."

"Prime Minister? Mrs. Williams?" A couple of press photographers called to her, and pasting a smile on her face, she knelt and posed with Ben.

Adeline took a photograph as well. Jasmine would never believe her otherwise.

"How about you stand in the picture, too?" The Prime Minister moved closer to her.

A red beam blinded her before sliding down her face to her chest. She twisted slightly and posed for the photographers with the Prime Minister and Ben.

Then Prime Minister Williams moved back in front of Adeline and held out a hand again. "Thank you—"

A flash came from the building across the road.

The Prime Minister jerked, shock written across her face.

There was another flash.

Something red erupted from the Prime Minister's

chest. Her hand started to rise to cover it. Then she fell forwards, landing on Adeline.

The phone jerked from her hand and fell to the ground, the camera going off again. Automatically, she cradled the injured woman, landing on the pavement with her. Pain filled her as her arm took the full weight of them both.

Police and security personnel swarmed from all directions. Chaos reigned around her. People's mouths opened and closed as they moved in slow motion. More flashes, something whizzed past her.

Nate landed on top of her, his breath hot against her ear, as he shielded her and the Prime Minister with his body.

6

Adeline lay stunned, unable to react as Nate finally rolled off her. Someone took the Prime Minister from her arms, and laid her on the ground. She sat up and grabbed her phone, putting it away, before she cradled her arm. Ben stood protectively next to her, one paw on her lap. In a daze she watched as a cop felt the Prime Minister's neck for a pulse, then shook his head. Another cop started CPR.

Someone touched her arm and she jumped, crying out. Her head snapped around, not letting her guard down even after she realized it was Nate.

"...with me now."

She shook her head. "I'm sorry. I didn't catch all of that."

"I said we have to get you away from here. I need you to come with me now."

"All right." She let him help her stand and took hold of Ben's lead. "Where are you taking me?"

"The station. You'll be safe—" He turned his face away.

Unable to make out the rest of what he said, Adeline turned back to look at the prone figure lying on the ground, blood spilling from her body in an ever growing flood. Paramedics worked ceaselessly on the motionless woman, counting aloud as they did.

Tears filled Adeline's eyes. Her whole body shook, and she glanced down, seeing the blood on her hands and clothes.

Lord God, be with Mrs. Williams' family right now. Preserve her life, but if it's Your will to take her, then take her now, don't let the paramedics try too long. Be with the government and security services as they try to make some sense from this. And be with the whole country as we come to terms with this horrific act.

Nate gripped her elbow firmly, as he ran to a marked police car, pulling her with him. Pain soared though her arm. She swallowed hard as nausea rose. Stars danced in front of her eyes. She tripped and would have fallen had he not held her.

"Please..." She needed to slow down. But in the chaos reigning around them, she wasn't sure if Nate even heard her, never mind responded, because he kept his face averted as he ran.

They reached the car and he put her inside, then climbed in. The car pulled away before she'd even had time to do up her seatbelt. Adeline closed her eyes, blissfully shutting herself off from the turmoil around her.

I don't want to believe what just happened. Someone shot the Prime Minister. They shot her right in front of me. It could have been me...was it meant to be me? It can't be. She's an important woman. I'm a no one.

The journey was short. She wasn't sure if that was a blessing or not. As soon as the car stopped, Nate touched her arm. He leapt out of the car and ran around the other side.

Once inside the safety of the police station, he led her to one of the interview rooms and sat her down. "Stay there. I'll get someone to look at your arm."

"I have to get back to work."

He shook his head. "No. You stay here." He

moved back to the door.

Adeline pulled out her phone. She texted Jasmine. *'Jas. The PM got shot. Not sure when I'll be back. Put news on. Think she's dead.'*

She slid the phone back into her pocket and looked around for Nate. He stood in the doorway talking to one of the other officers. Adeline watched his face. "...tea and then I'll talk to her. No, I'll do it. She was right next to Mrs. Williams when she was shot. Get Dane to ring Jas and ask her to..." He turned away and she couldn't see any more.

Tears filled her eyes, and she looked down at Ben. He licked her hand and wagged his tail. He always knew when she was upset and tried to cheer her up. "I know, buddy," she told him. "Me too." She was caught in some kind of a nightmare. The phone in her pocket vibrated and she pulled it out. The caller ID read Jasmine. She answered. "Hey, Jas."

She read the reply. "What's going on? The news is chaotic. They're saying the Prime Minister is critical."

"Yeah. I was right next to her. I caught her when she fell."

"What? Are you hurt? Where are you?"

"I'm at the police station with Nate. Dane's around somewhere—" She broke off seeing blood on her hands.

Shaking hard, she looked down at herself. Blood lay thick and heavy over her white coat. The Prime Minister's blood. She dropped the phone, nausea rising. A strangled cry rose up and out before she could stop it. Trembling fingers tried to undo the coat buttons, but failed.

Ben nudged her leg. Black shoes appeared on the edge of her field of vision. Strong hands covered hers, helping her. She glanced up into Nate's concerned face. He undid her coat and pulled it off. She cried out in pain as her arm moved awkwardly.

"Take a couple of deep breaths. We'll need the coat for now. I'll get a doc in here to check you over, then you can go and clean up before we take your statement."

Adeline nodded slightly. Her skirt was stained, too. "I dropped my phone."

He picked it up and handed it to her. "There you go."

"Thank you. I should get back to work." There was something she needed to tell him, something important, but what was it?

"You can't leave until you've given a statement. Things are a little hectic right now, but..." he turned away, and Adeline lost the rest of what he said.

She closed her eyes, trying to stop shaking. *I wish I knew what was happening out there. Is she dead? How much chaos is there? Let them catch the guy quickly.*

Was it too much of a coincidence that the guy who'd bought the doll in to be mended, had vanished into a building in the same direction the shots came from? She scrolled through the photos on her phone. There was the man and there was the building. That was it. Him.

She almost dropped the handset again as she twisted around. "Nate?"

Nate turned back to her. "Yes?"

"I've seen him before. He came into the shop. And then he went into this building right before the shooting. I took his photo."

He moved swiftly over to her and took the phone. "This man here?"

Adeline nodded. "Yes. That's what I was trying to tell you before all this happened."

"I'll be back. Don't you go anywhere. I need to keep this as evidence for now. You'll get it back."

"I need my phone to talk to people. It's got particular software on it. I can't just use any old phone."

"You'll get it back or we'll give you a replacement." He strode rapidly over to the door.

Despite the situation, for a moment, she found herself admiring his authoritative stance. Then frustration at having her means of communicating long distance taken away set back in.

Adeline glanced down at Ben and sighed. Maybe she said the wrong thing again. Her hands were sticky with blood and she longed to go and wash them.

A hand dropped on her shoulder and she jumped. "Oh…"

"Hi, I'm Dr. Chandler. I'm the police surgeon. I didn't mean to startle you." The woman was blonde and her eyes carried her smile behind the glasses. "I need to check you over."

Her arm hurt like the blazes, but in the grand scheme of things, it just didn't matter. "I'm fine. Just need to clean up."

Dr. Chandler took her hands, causing her to gasp in pain, and started to examine them. "…samples…"

"I can't hear you," Adeline said. "I'm deaf. If you look at me when you speak, I can lip read."

The blonde woman frowned. "I'm sorry, I didn't realize. I said I'll need to take samples of the blood from your hands and under your nails. But that gasp of pain tells me you're not fine. Where does it hurt?"

"My arm's a little sore from where I fell, but that's

not important, right now. How's the Prime Minister?"

"She didn't make it."

Shock resonated through Adeline, setting every nerve on edge. She swallowed hard, bile rising as if someone had thumped her hard in the stomach. Thinking and guessing that was the outcome, was vastly different to seeing it spoken. She closed her eyes, blocking herself off completely from the world. The silence surrounding her became a blessing.

She couldn't be dead. They needed her, with the fragile state the country was in at the moment. She was the only woman who could unite the country and lead them out of the recession. She was their one hope and now she was gone.

They'd been working on her when Nate brought her here. She might have died in her arms.

Hot tears streamed down Adeline's face, huge choking sobs welled up and out. Falling to her knees, she wrapped her arms around her stomach, rocking back and forth.

A wet nose nudged her arm a fraction before strong arms wrapped around her, the scent of mint and aftershave following it. A hand moved slowly over her back in an attempt to both comfort and console. *Nate...*

Not opening her eyes, she took the comfort he offered.

After a few minutes, he tapped her shoulder, and she opened her eyes. She held his gaze, wanting him to tell her it wasn't true. "Nate, she can't be dead. They were working on her. She has to be all right."

"I'm sorry, but it's true. Mrs. Williams is dead. They just made the official announcement." He took a deep breath. "Are you all right? The doc wanted to sedate you, but I intervened."

"Thank you. I'm fine. I need to know if she…" She took a deep breath. "Did she die in my arms?"

Nate didn't answer until she repeated her question. Then he nodded. "Yes. I'm sorry."

A fresh wave of tears fell down her cheeks. The Prime Minister had given birth to her first child, a daughter, only a few weeks previously. This was her first official engagement on her return to work. She'd never get to hold the baby again or sing to her. And the baby would never know her mother.

"Let the doc check you over," he said. "Jas is coming in with a change of clothes for you. We'll need the ones you have on as evidence. Then, once we've taken a statement, I'll drive you home."

"All right." Adeline took a deep shuddering breath, wanting to wipe her eyes, but not wanting to get blood on her face. She settled for wiping her sleeve over them and then looked at the doctor.

Dr. Chandler smiled. "This won't take long. Sergeant, if you'll excuse us please."

He looked at her and nodded. "Sure. I'll be right outside."

Adeline gripped his arm tightly. "Stay." She needed a familiar face, one friendly presence in the midst of the horror.

Nate turned to face the doctor for a long moment, then smiled at her. "Sure." He sat next to her.

Dr. Chandler scrapped under Adeline's nails while Adeline blinked hard and glanced at Nate. His lips moved in what was obviously a prayer. She prayed along with him. Once it was over and the doctor had left, Jasmine came into the room.

Her friend held out a bag. "I got you some clothes like Dane asked." She dropped the bag and held out her arms.

"I don't want to get blood on you."

"Never mind about that. You need a hug."

"Yes, I do." Adeline hugged Jasmine tightly. "Thank you."

Jasmine hugged her then pulled back. She gently ran a hand down Adeline's face, before signing as she spoke. "Are you sure you're all right?"

Adeline shrugged. She glanced at Nate and Dane standing on the other side of the room and signed her reply. She knew Nate could follow some of her signing now, but didn't want to verbalize how she felt. "No, I'm not all right. Jas, Mrs. Williams died in my arms."

Jasmine's eyes widened as she replied rapidly in sign. "Seriously?"

"She stopped right by me, petted Ben, spoke to me. She had her picture taken with me and Ben. Then she got shot and landed on me. Jas, I was the last person to touch her, to speak to her."

"I am so sorry, hon," Jasmine signed and hugged her tightly. Then pulling back, she sighed. "Dane wants me to go, so he and Nate can interview you. I'll go back to your house and put a casserole in the oven for you."

Adeline shook her head. "Thank you, but I'm not hungry."

"I know you're not, but you still need to eat. I'm doing it. Call if you need me to come around later. Remember I love you." She hugged her again and then headed out.

"Love you too," Adeline called after her. She raised a hand in farewell and then looked down at the bag of clothes. "Can I go and change?"

Nate nodded "I'll show you."

"Thank you." She followed him down the hallway.

Ten minutes later, she came out of the ladies room. Nate was leaning against the wall, waiting. She'd managed to wash off all of the blood, but longed for a hot shower. She could still feel it clinging to her. This must be how Lady Macbeth felt in the Shakespeare play.

"Feeling better?"

She nodded, resisting the temptation to ask him if he spent a lot of time hanging around outside the ladies. He looked well practiced at it, but then he *was* usually accompanied on trips by Vianne. Now just wasn't the time for humor. "Yeah."

"All right. Let's go back to the interview room so we can take a statement."

"Nate...first there is something you and Dane need to know. I tried telling you earlier, but everything was so chaotic. I've seen him before."

He tilted his head. "Who?"

"The shooter. He came into the doll hospital this morning, but that's not important. Nate, he's the man from my nightmares. The one with the ponytail."

Nate's gaze turned to stone. "He's what?"

"I think he's the Herbalist."

7

Adeline cradled the mug of steaming tea in both hands. Nate, Dane, and their commanding officer, DI Welsh, along with an MI5 officer whose name she didn't remember, sat opposite her. She gazed down at her cup. Ben sat by her feet, his tail thudding against her leg. Long slender fingers moved under her field of vision and she slowly raised her head. "I'm sorry, I don't remember anything else. It all happened so fast."

Nate slid a picture over to her. "We took this from your phone. What can you tell us about this man?"

"He came into the doll hospital this morning. He had a broken doll with him, wanted me to mend it immediately."

"What was wrong with the doll?"

"The arm had come off. It's easy enough to reattach with the right tools. It took me five minutes. He was on edge the whole time."

"Did he give you a name?"

Adeline let go of the cup, signing as she spoke. "No, we don't need one as we don't keep records for walk-ins. And he paid cash. I did him a receipt but he didn't take it." She jabbed a finger at the picture. "Actually, he over-paid, so the receipt is for what he gave me. He paced and watched out the window. I thought he must just be in a hurry. There was something about him and the way he kept looking at me. As if he could see straight through me, knew who I was."

"Did you recognize him?"

"Not at first. Yes, he had a ponytail, but it was blond, not black, and a lot of guys do their hair like that these days. It was only after he left that I realized who the eyes reminded me of."

"So you followed him?" Nate's eyes bored into hers, signing the words he knew. "You didn't think to call me or Dane, or just dial the station?"

She pushed the cup away, spilling hot tea over her hands. "No, you're wrong. I tried calling you, but you didn't answer. So, I sent a text, but you never replied. We assumed you were caught up on a case and would get back to me when you could. Then Jas suggested I take Ben for a walk and head to the memorial garden to see the Prime Minister and clear my head. She said that I might see you out there. I told her that you wouldn't be doing street duty, but you were there."

Her painful hands shook as she wiped them on her sleeves. "I'm not stupid. I wasn't going to follow him on my own. If it is him…" She broke off. "Something I just remembered. There was a red light, like a laser."

The MI5 guy raised his hand. "When?"

"Before the Prime Minister got shot. The light blinded me then slid to my chest as we posed for the photographers. Then the Prime Minister moved in front of me just as she got shot. The flash came from the building this man went in to."

The four officers exchanged a long look. Then the MI5 officer turned back to her. "You're sure the light hit you and not Mrs. Williams?"

"She was standing next to me, but the light was on me. I turned so it wouldn't blind me."

She buried her head in her hands, struggling with the grief and fear forcing its way through her. Tears filled her eyes, and she closed them, shutting herself off from everyone in the room. Her shoulders shook. Could she have been the target and not the Prime Minister? The thought was too stupid and hideous to contemplate. She had simply been in the wrong place at the wrong time.

Sudden images flooded her mind. The red sheen dropped and engulfed her.

A ponytail whipped around slapping her face, and a hand clamped over her mouth. The stench of garlic flooded her senses. She struggled to breathe, her hands rising to her throat, trying to push away the knife. Hot breath rasped against her ear, fingers traced the pulse point in her neck, before steel met skin in a final blow.

"Noooooooo......"

Almost immediately, Nate vaulted the table, his arms going around her. She clung to him like an anchor in a storm. Dimly aware of the vibrations in his throat, she knew he was speaking, but wasn't sure who to. It didn't matter. The Herbalist had struck again, and they were no nearer to catching him.

After a moment she looked up, her vision blurred with the tears, which fell unrestrained. She caught Nate's gaze and held it. "The Herbalist. Again," she managed.

"Where?"

"I don't know. There was a hallway, green carpet, but I couldn't breathe. He put a knife to my throat. The stench of the garlic..."

The MI5 agent tapped her arm. "Let me get this straight, Miss Monroe. You just zoned out. Are you telling me you 'see' these murders?"

Adeline nodded mutely. His disdain and disbelief was evident in his eyes and facial expression, without her needing to hear it.

She caught the look Dane gave him. "She knows things we haven't released to the press. And we've seen her visions before. Each time she's been right. The only thing we're unsure of is the timing. Do they happen at the same time as she sees them, or before? Either way we take her seriously and suggest you do the same."

DI Welsh stood and headed from the room. Adeline watched her go and then turned to Nate, her whole body still shaking. "You need to get someone out there."

"The Guv's getting uniform officers out into the herb roads and surrounding streets. Hopefully flooding the area will catch him."

****

As Nate drove though the now deserted streets, Adeline sat in the front seat of his car, with Ben curled up in the back. She angled herself so she could see his lips. "Thank you for driving me home."

"It's not a problem."

"I still don't believe it."

"Nor me."

"It's like something out of a nightmare." The car pulled to the curb outside her house. She reached down for her bag. "Thank you for the lift."

"You're welcome, Adeline. Do you want me to come in for a while?"

"No. I'll be fine. Thanks for the offer, but you should get home to Vianne. Jas said she'd come back later on." She exited the car and opened the door for Ben. "Thanks again."

"Welcome."

She walked up the path, Ben running at her heels. The front door blew open. "That's strange. Jas would have shut and locked the door behind her. Go on ahead, Ben. Go see what's wrong." She let go of the lead.

As she reached the doorstep, a hand touched her arm and she jumped. She turned to see Nate. "I thought you'd gone."

"No, I was waiting to make sure you got in safely. Stay here."

"Nate…"

"Just stay here." Nate followed Ben up the step and pushed open the front door fully.

Ben backed away, his ears down and his tail between his legs.

Nate staggered backwards, his hand over his mouth.

Adeline's stomach twisted. She stood on her tiptoes trying to see over Nate's shoulder.

Jasmine lay in the hallway, blood draining from the knife wound in her throat. A gaping chasm appeared under Adeline's feet, and she dropped to her knees, retching, losing the tea she'd drunk at the police station.

The vision she'd had. It was her hallway. It had been Jasmine's death she'd seen.

Noooo…not Jas. Why?

She closed her eyes, shutting herself off in the tsunami of anguish and devastation rushing through her. Strong arms enfolded her, but she didn't move or open her eyes as she knew it was Nate from the spearmint and musk. A huge lump in her throat made breathing difficult.

After a minute or two, Nate gently lifted her face to his. "Adeline, I need you to stay here a minute. I'll be right back. And I mean stay right here."

There was no way she could move any way at that precise moment.

He left her momentarily as he checked pointlessly for Jasmine's pulse and then shook his head. "I'm sorry." He returned and pulled her upright. "Let's get you away from here."

He wrapped his arm around her waist and moved her away from the house. She walked remotely, turning her head back to look at the house. She could see Jasmine lying in the hallway. Tears stung her eyes as she finally pulled her gaze away.

Leading her to the car Nate unlocked the door and sat her on the front seat.

Adeline sat sideways in the seat, her feet on the pavement, as Nate pulled out his phone and dialed rapidly. "Guv, it's Nate. I need a full forensic team and an ambulance..." He turned away, his face ashen.

Tears streaming down her face, Adeline buried her face in her hands. *God, why Jasmine? Haven't enough people died today without any more?*

Blue lights filled the dark night. Leather clad feet rushed past her. Crime scene lights flashed on as a white tent was set up over the front of the house.

A hand closed over her arm, the touch firm and she looked up, her vision blurred with her tears. "Nate... what about Dane?"

"The Guv is going to tell him. I need to take you someplace else. Where can you go tonight that's safe?"

"Forget me. Dane needs to know before the news

breaks. Jas is his wife."

"DI Welsh is on her way to tell him. In cases like this, the highest ranking officer—"

She shook her head, putting her finger over his lips. "He's your partner. She was your friend, my best friend. It should come from you."

Several emotions flashed across Nate's face before he finally nodded. His eyes, filled with pain and anguish, glistened in the street light. "All right. I'll get a uniformed officer to drive you. Just tell me where."

"My brother Mark's house," she whispered.

"Where does he live?"

"Fifteen Highgrove Crescent. It's on the other side of town. My parents are staying there for a couple of days before they go on holiday tomorrow. I can't go too far away. I need to be here for work."

It was strange how her mind functioned. Even with all that had happened today, first the Prime Minister being assassinated and now Jasmine dying, part of her worried about the doll's hospital. She couldn't let the children down.

"All right." He helped her to her feet.

"I'll need some things first..."

He shook his head. "I can't let you back in there. It's a crime scene." He led her to a different patrol car and settled her inside it. "I'll swing by and see you on my way home if it's not too late." He shut the door.

Adeline looked towards her house. Blue lights reflected off the windows. Police officers moved in and out and two white suited figures lingered by the white tent covering her porch. It was like a TV program. CSI Headley Cross on her doorstep.

****

PC Burnett escorted her to the doorway of Mark's three-story town house. He pushed the doorbell. Adeline just hoped and prayed Mark or someone was in. She had nowhere else to go if there wasn't. Lights blazed from upstairs, but that didn't mean anything. Being in the army and working shifts, Mark was very security conscious and kept all the lights and even the TV on a timer switch.

A shadow appeared at the glass panel and the door opened. "Addie. Talk about timing. We've been trying to call you for hours. Dad was just about to drive over to your place and check on you." Mark's face creased in concern as he took in the police officer standing next to her. "Addie—is everything all right?"

She shook her head, her hands jerking as she signed. "Jasmine's dead. She was killed in my house. I have nowhere to go. Can I...?"

"Oh, no, hon. I'm so sorry. Of course you can stay." Grief crossed Mark's face as he pulled her into his arms. She buried her face in his sweater, assuming the police officer was explaining about Jasmine. Was he mentioning the Prime Minister as well, or did Mark and her parents already know about her involvement? Why else would her dad be about to drive over to her place?

Lord, be with Dane and the girls right now. As bad as I feel, they're going to feel so much worse.

Mark's chest vibrated as he spoke, and Adeline glanced up at his face. "... can stay here as long as she needs. I've been really worried about her since the news about the Prime Minister. Her picture was right alongside Adeline's."

PC Burnett angled his face so Adeline could read

his lips. "Just keep her safe tonight. DS Holmes and Agent Debone from MI5 will need to talk to her again in the morning."

Adeline drew in a deep shuddering breath. "Thank you for bringing me here, Officer."

He nodded. "You're welcome. Goodnight."

Mark held her tightly as he shut the front door. "Adeline, I'm so sorry about Jasmine. And with the Prime Minister being killed like that today. When I saw you on the news standing right next to her, I just…I was scared something had happened to you. Perhaps you'd got shot, too. No one would tell us anything and you weren't answering your phone…"

Safe in her brother's arms, Adeline started to shake as the full impact of the day's events hit her.

Mark led her into the lounge and her parents stood. His chest rumbled as he spoke, presumably explaining quickly.

"Mum…Dad…" Tears fell as they surrounded her, the four of them standing together. After a moment she pulled away so she could follow the conversation.

"Are you hurt?" Her mother asked.

"My arm's a little sore, but I'm OK, Mum."

"We were really worried," her father added. "Especially when you didn't answer your phone."

"The police have it as evidence, Dad."

"Are you sure you're OK?"

"No, no, I'm not. My best friend is dead, I need…" her voice broke, but she continued. "The Prime Minister…we needed her..."

"That's an understatement. You're all over the news, sis." Mark signed as he spoke. "Would you feel up to talking about it?"

"Jasmine or the Prime Minister?"

"Either, both…"

"OK." She wasn't sure she wanted to talk, but knowing Mark he'd want details, as would her dad. However her mother would only worry if she knew everything. And if she started talking about visions, they'd think she was insane.

Lord, help me here. Let me get the balance right between what they need to know and what they don't. Like Nate keeps saying, it's an active case. Albeit one that's now hit way too close to home.

Dad looked at her. "But first we pray," he said. "Then we talk."

"Pray for Dane," she signed. "Nate's gone to tell him and the girls about Jas."

****

Nate's body, cold and numb, moved on autopilot as he drove to Dane's house. Too much had happened today, and he still had the worst part to come. Some days he loved his job, and other times he hated it. Today fell into the latter category. Bad news was never easy, but this—

He parked the car and buried his face in his hands. *Lord, give me the words. I'm about to shatter Dane's life—to shred his future into thousands of tiny pieces and toss them into the air for the wind to blow away like chaff.*

A car door shut behind him as he got out of his car. His boss headed down to meet him. She looked like she'd been crying, but being a gentleman, Nate didn't say anything. "I'm not looking forward to this, Guv."

"Nor me. How are you doing?"

Nate shrugged. "Not great, but coping so far. I'll

go home and have a bath and early night. There's a lot of work to do tomorrow."

"Where did you send Miss Monroe?"

"She's with her brother and parents." Nate rubbed a hand over his face. "She's devastated. Not only did the Prime Minister die in her arms, she goes home to find Jas...." He turned the crack in his voice into a cough. The last person he wanted to lose it in front of was his boss. "I'll talk to her again in the morning."

"No, you won't. I want you to take tomorrow off."

"With all due respect, stuff that, ma'am. I don't need to sit at home, moping. I want, *need*, to be out on the streets trying to find Jas's killer. Plus, the Herbalist is still out there. Even if he did kill the Prime Minister, which we still don't know for sure one way or the other, it's my case."

"MI5 have jurisdiction on the assassination." DI Welsh fixed her piercing blue eyes on him. "And you are taking tomorrow off. That's an order."

"Guv, please. Yes, there's a chance it's the same guy, but it's possible it isn't. I owe it to Jas and Dane to look into this. She's one of our own."

"Nate. You know the rules. You are personally involved now. And I don't just mean Jasmine. There's a certain witness you're getting friendly with. Overly friendly."

Nate's heart stopped. "Guv, there is nothing going on with Ade—"

"Thank you." She looked at him. "I wish you'd told me sooner, rather than leaving it to me to work it out."

Had he protested too much and too fast? He pushed his fingers through his hair. "Adeline and I are friends. Nothing more than that. At least not right now."

"I don't want anything to jeopardize this case, Nate. If it goes to court and it comes out that you've been fraternizing with one of the witnesses, it's not going to look good."

"*When* it comes to court, not if, because I *will* catch him."

DI Welsh frowned. "Very well, *when* it goes to court, I don't want the defense playing on any relationship going on between the star witness and the investigating copper. Because that will dead stick any case we have faster than superglue."

"There won't be. We know each other from church. She's fixed Vianne's dolls a couple of times. She's a witness. And a friend. That's all."

"Are you sure?"

He paused for a moment, remembering the blistering kiss he and Adeline had shared. He'd bolted afterwards, acutely aware of the line he'd crossed. It couldn't happen again. Somehow he had to keep her at arm's length, at least for now. But with each passing minute, it was getting harder and harder to do. "I'm sure. But this isn't about me. My partner's wife has just been murdered. He needs my support and I need to help find the guy who did this." He paused, rubbing his hands over his arms in the chill night air. "And you know as well as I do that Adeline saw this one. It's too much of a coincidence for it not to have been the Herbalist. Therefore Dane also witnessed it, the same as I did. Don't tell me I can't get out there tomorrow and hunt down this creep. Because one way or the other I will do it anyway. I'd rather do it with your blessing."

DI Welsh sighed. She brushed a hand over her

face. "Fine...but you keep me in the loop and you don't step on MI5's toes. They won't like it."

Nate nodded as he rang the doorbell. Sweat covered his palms, bile rose in his throat, and his stomach cramped. As he prayed for peace and the strength to do this, he hopped from one foot to the other.

A small shadow ran down the hallway and flung open the door. Jodie looked at him, her face falling slightly. "Oh, Uncle Nate. I thought it was mummy without her door key. She's always forgetting it. Daddy says he's going to put it on a chain around her neck before he's much older."

Nate somehow managed to find a smile for her. "Hey, Jodie. Is Daddy here?"

Jodie nodded. "He's burning dinner in the kitchen. And getting all stressy with it." She opened the door wide to let them in.

Nate headed down the hall to the kitchen, his boss at his side.

Dane stood by the sink, straining a pan of potatoes into the colander. His voice floated across to them. "Did you forget your keys again, Jas? How's Adeline doing? She was pretty shaken—" His voice died as he turned and saw Nate and his boss standing there.

The pan fell from his hand, hitting the floor, boiling water and potatoes spilling everywhere. Color drained from his cheeks and his face cracked. "No...."

Nate turned to Jodie. "Take Vicky in the lounge for a minute while we help Daddy clean up. Don't want you getting hurt." He watched Jodie take her sister's hand and leave the room. Then he moved over to his partner. "Dane, I'm sorry."

"No, no, no. I don't want to hear it. She's fine.

She's at Adeline's." Dane's gaze flicked desperately from Nate's face to DI Welsh's and back.

"There was an incident at Adeline's," Nate said quietly, his own heart breaking as he destroyed his partner's world.

"*Incident*?" Dane spat the word back at him. "What do you mean an *incident*?"

"After we left the station, I took Adeline home. The front door was open, and we found Jas in the hallway. She's dead, Dane. I'm so sorry."

Dane's eyes widened, and he arched forwards as if he'd been punched hard in the stomach. His hands clenched and unclenched, before he swept everything off the worktop onto the floor in one sweep. "No," he yelled, his voice cracking.

Nate moved over to him, grabbing his arms. "Stop it."

"Let go of me," Dane roared, struggling free and sweeping the plates from the table to the floor.

Nate grabbed him, pulling him to his chest and not letting go. "Dane, stop it. She's gone. Destroying the kitchen isn't going to bring her back."

Tears ran down Dane's face. "Jasmine...why did God take her when I need her?"

"I don't know," Nate whispered, tears burning his own eyes.

"How did she die? You saw her, tell me how she died."

"I can't tell you any more than I already have."

"Don't give me that," Dane yelled. "You just told me you found her. How. Did. She. Die?"

Nate sucked in a long breath. "Her throat was cut."

Dane let out an almost animal scream of pain.

"Nooooooo."

DI Welsh's phone rang. She pulled it from her pocket. "Welsh…I see. All right, thank you." She snapped it shut and looked at the two men. "You interrupted the killer."

"What?" Nate shook his head. "We can't have. There was no one else in the house. I'd have seen them leave."

"Jasmine had a packet of ivy in her pocket. It was the Herbalist. He hadn't had time to move the body."

Dane struggled, trying to get away. "No. It wasn't her murder I sat and listened to in that interview room." He hit out at Nate. "It wasn't her."

Nate warded off the blows. He glanced at the door as Jodie appeared.

"Daddy, Vicky won't…what's wrong with Daddy?"

DI Welsh moved over to her. "Jodie, isn't it? I need your help. Do you know your grandma's phone number?" She took the child's hand and led her from the room.

Nate didn't let go of Dane, sinking to the floor with him as Dane's knees gave way, finally giving in to his own sorrow.

When the DI came back in, the first storm of grief had passed. Both men sat on the floor, knees against their chests and wrists resting on their knees. DI Welsh sat on the floor opposite them. "I've called your parents, Dane. They're coming over."

"Thanks." Dane's voice shuddered out, his rage spent. "Are you sure it was him? I mean…"

DI Welsh nodded. "The ivy, the MO, it all fits. And her injuries are consistent with what Miss Monroe described in the interview room." She fixed her gaze on Nate. "I think he was after Miss Monroe. What's her brother's address?"

"Fifteen Highgrove Crescent. We can't ring her as we still have her phone as evidence."

"I'll make sure she gets it back in the morning or we get her a replacement. I'm putting an officer outside her brother's house tonight. I'm not waiting on MI5 to make a decision about protective custody."

"I need to call Jas's parents," Dane's voice was no more than a broken whisper. His shoulders slumped as he glanced up. He looked fifteen years older than he had twenty minutes ago.

"I'll drive over there and tell them myself," DI Welsh said. "Your parents will be here any minute." She stood up and dropped a hand on Dane's shoulder. "If there is anything I can do, let me know."

"You can catch the man who killed my wife, lock him up, and throw away the key. That's what you can do."

"That's a given," she promised. "Where do Jas's parents live?"

"Twenty Stonebridge Close."

"OK. I'll head over there now. I'm really sorry."

"Thanks."

Her footsteps clicked across the floor, and the front door opened and closed.

Dane groaned. "What do I tell the girls? How do I tell them mummy isn't coming home?"

"I don't know. But I know Someone who does." Nate turned to his friend and partner and wrapping his arms around him, began to pray.

8

Adeline pushed her spoon through the bowl of cereal, her eyes following the closed captions on the television. Her picture was plastered all over the breakfast news, right alongside the Prime Minister's.

Every time she'd closed her eyes during the night, she had seen Mrs. Williams fall against her over and over again. Those images had blurred and mixed with the ones of Jasmine lying dead in Adeline's hallway.

She glanced out of the kitchen window at the police car. She remembered them arriving very late in the evening. Mark had talked with them and hadn't told her what they wanted. Just the fact they were parked there spoke volumes. She was obviously being protected from something.

As she watched, the MI5 agent from the previous day arrived and exchanged a few words with the police. The panda car drove off to be replaced by a black sedan.

She put the spoon down. The sedan screamed unmarked police car just as loudly as the stripes and lights yelled police car.

She pushed the bowl away.

"You need to eat something." Her mother gently pushed the bowl back.

"I'm really not hungry, Mum."

"None of us are, darling. But, Jasmine wouldn't want you getting sick on her account."

"OK." She took a couple more mouthfuls.

Her dad came in with the morning paper. "It's chaos in the newsagents," he said laying the paper on the table. "And as for the grocery store, forget it. No milk left already. You'll need to run over to the supermarket later on and get some, Adeline."

"OK, Dad. I will."

"Anyone would think it was Christmas, it's so busy. Talk about panic buying."

Her mother nodded. "It was like that after Princess Diana died, David, do you remember?"

Adeline tuned out her parent's conversation. She rose and turned off the television, not wanting to see news of Jasmine's murder. They were concentrating on the death of the Prime Minister for the moment, but the local news was due on any moment. The Deputy Prime Minister was making a statement in an hour followed by an emergency debate in the House of Commons. She caught a glimpse of the morning newspaper. Her picture with the Prime Minister had pride of place on the front cover. Right next to the black edged photo of the Prime Minister on her own, and beneath that the one of the two of them with Ben.

Mark came into the kitchen in his uniform.

She managed a faint smile. "Love the new insignia," she told him. She flashed off a mock salute. "Lieutenant-Colonel looks good on you, bro."

Mark smiled. "Thank you, sis. When I get called that, I automatically look around for someone else. I need to sew them onto my dress uniform and my class A's."

"If you like I'll sew them on for you."

He signed as he spoke. "That would be great. Thanks. The uniforms are in the wardrobe, and the insignias in the box on the dresser. I have to go soon. We're going to be flat out today. I wish I didn't have to go. I'd rather stay here with you."

"I'll be fine. I have Ben."

"It's not the same. I should be here. You shouldn't be alone right now. Not after yesterday."

"Really, I'll be all right."

"But Mum and Dad are leaving on the cruise today. You'll only have Ben for company."

"I just don't feel right about leaving." Her mother placed her hand over Adeline's arm. "We were thinking of cancelling—"

Adeline cut her mother off. "Don't you dare cancel the cruise. You've been looking forward to this trip for months."

"You need us here."

"You need this holiday. I'll be here when you get back."

Her mother looked at her. "But, sweetie, you need me here more than we need a holiday."

Adeline scowled. "Mum, you can't. You'll lose all that money. You and Dad saved for years for this trip. It's the chance of a lifetime, and I won't let you throw it away. If you cancel it won't bring Jasmine back."

Then she changed tactics. "Please…Jas wouldn't want you to miss out on her account." She deliberately quoted her mother's words back at her. "I promise, I'll be fine. Anyway, the taxi is due here at any time. It's too late to cancel."

Her mother's brow furrowed as she waivered. Worry, grief and concern danced in her mother's eyes and she twisted her wedding ring. A sure sign she was conflicted about something.

Adeline tried one last tack. "I'll text you every day.

At least once every six hours. And if I don't, Ben will." She tilted her head. "Did I tell you I've been teaching him how to use the phone?"

"OK." She relented after a long pause. "But if you need us, call and we'll come right home." Her mother hugged her.

Adeline returned the hug. "Thank you."

Mark hesitated, his face contorting with conflicting emotions. "Addie, I'm not sure…"

Adeline held his gaze. "Don't you get on my case as well. I know you love me and want to protect me, but right now I just want to sew your insignia on your uniforms. The police are right outside. Then I have to call Dane to see how he and the girls are doing this morning. I should ring Susie, tell her to go in and open up and maybe I'll go into work for a little bit."

"Work? Are you crazy?" He shook his head at her, repeating the signs twice.

"Maybe, but it's what I want to do."

"Fine, but if you need anything, you call me. I am never too busy for you, Adeline."

"Thank you." She hugged him tightly. "You always wanted a famous sister," she joked.

"Not like this, hon. Not like this."

She sat down again, listlessly playing with her breakfast. She glanced up as Mark sat opposite her. "I'm sorry. I'm not hungry."

His hand covered hers, his touch warm against her cold skin. "It's fine."

Ben jumped up, touched Adeline's leg and ran to the door. Mark smiled. "That's someone at the door. Be right back."

Adeline grabbed her bowl and carried it to the sink to wash it. She took pleasure in the water enveloping her hands, washing away…everything. It was hot against her cold, clammy fingers. The bubbles sat in the palm of her hands and coated the backs of them. For a moment normality existed. Nothing bad had happened.

Who am I trying to kid? I can't even manage to eat a bowl of cereal this morning.

Although Mark was an amazing cook, she'd refused his offer of bacon and eggs, and even turned down his suggestion of pancakes. Jasmine was dead. Breakfast wouldn't fix that. Nothing could. Nothing would ever be the same again.

She turned around and leaned against the counter. Her parents came in wearing coats.

"The taxi's here," her father said.

She hugged him and then her mother. "Have a great time. Email me lots of photos. And don't worry too much. Everything will be fine."

Her mother still didn't look convinced. "Three months is a long time."

"You'll be too busy having fun to worry about me. Shuffleboard on the deck, walks on the prom, dinner at the Captain's table to name a few. Oh, and don't forget all those men in uniform."

Her mother laughed. "Take care."

"You too." She raised a hand and waved as they headed into the hall. She turned back to the sink, finishing the dishes slowly. She swallowed hard, trying to push off the feeling that she wasn't going to see them again. *Now you're being stupid. Of course you're seeing them again. In three months' time they'll be back, bronzed and well rested. Stop being pathetic.*

Ben nudged her and she looked down, drying her hands on the tea towel. "What is it?" She followed his gaze to the door. Mark stood there with Nate and the MI5 bloke from the previous day. Her heart pounded as she took in the black suit, shirt and tie Nate wore. With huge dark circles under his red rimmed eyes, he didn't look like he'd gotten much sleep, either.

"Morning, Nate." She wasn't going to say good morning. There was nothing good about it by any stretch of the imagination.

Nate looked at her, a slight smile on his lips that never quite reached his eyes. He moved over to her and hugged her. "Morning, Adeline. How are you?"

"I've been better. How are you?"

Nate shrugged. "Been better. Guv told me to take the day off, but I need to be working. It's the least I can do for Dane and Jas."

"Have you seen Dane? How's he doing?"

"Dane's a mess. His parents have come to look after the girls, but he's not coping at all."

"I didn't think he would be. Just wish there was more I could do to help them."

"So do I. I saw your parents leave in a taxi. Where are they going?"

"Three month cruise of the Caribbean. Mum wanted to cancel, but I talked her out of it. They've been planning this for months. And Jas would want them to go."

"Yeah, she would." He broke off. "You remember Agent Debone?"

"Yes." She nodded and took in the stern appearance of the dark haired agent standing by her brother. So that's what his name was. She tried to block out the part of her mind that started singing *dem-bones* rather irreverently.

"I've come to take you to a safe house." Agent

Debone held her gaze.

Adeline shook her head. "I can stay here. I don't need to move."

"It's too dangerous for you to remain here."

She shoved her hands into her pockets, her shoulders stiffening. "No one knows where I am. Mark's in the army. He is more than capable of protecting me. As is Ben."

"Miss Monroe, Jasmine is dead. She died in your house."

"I know she's dead." Tears filled Adeline's eyes, and she brushed them away. "You don't need to remind me of that any more than I need to remind you who else died yesterday. But unless you can link the two cases, I either stay here or go home."

Agent Debone looked at her for a moment then turned his back and faced Mark.

"I can't read your lips when you do that."

He glanced back at her. "I'm not speaking to you."

Adeline threw her hands in the air with exasperation. Anger flashed through her and she tried to swallow it, but failed. "Fine. Not like this concerns me at all, is it? I'll go find your uniforms, Mark." She stormed to the door and flung it open so hard it bounced back off the wall as she flounced through it, heading to the stairs. Ben ran after her.

****

Nate watched her go, his stomach falling and then twisting as the door slammed shut, the sound reverberating around the kitchen. He'd argued the necessity to include Adeline in the discussion, but been shouted down, quite literally. "Should I go after her?"

Mark shook his head. "She's just very touchy about being deaf. She always has been. However, cutting her out of the conversation like that, Agent Debone, is just plain rude and that is uncalled for. Does she have to go into hiding? Did someone kill Jasmine instead of her? Or is this just because she was there when the Prime Minister died?"

Before Agent Debone could speak, Nate jumped in. "Can we link the two cases? Not yet. As far as Jasmine's death goes?" He paused for a moment. "Local papers have picked up that story. The Nationals have Adeline's photo all over them, along with the possibility she can ID the Prime Minister's killer."

Shock filled Mark's face. "Are you sure? I mean the news said..."

Nate held up a hand. "She took a photograph of him, saw him go into the building the shots were fired from. Unfortunately, the press got a hold of that information before we could issue a D notice. By the time we realized, it'd gone to print and was online." He paused. "As for Jas? She was murdered by the Herbalist. We got there before he had a chance to move the body."

Mark paled. "*What?* How do you know?"

"I can't tell you that, but we know for sure it was him. Adeline has given us a description of him. With her photo in the news, he'll know he got the wrong woman."

"Wait a minute..." Mark tugged down his camouflage jacket. "You're telling me that Adeline knows who this guy is, and he's after her?"

"It looks like it. We're moving her into a safe house before he tries again."

The door opened behind him. "What did I miss?"

Adeline asked.

Mark looked over Nate's shoulder, signing as he spoke. "They say the Herbalist killed Jasmine. That he might be coming for you. They want to put you in a safe house."

Nate turned around, seeing Adeline standing in the doorway, a pile of uniforms in her arms and a resolute look on her face that he knew all too well. Vianne used it a lot.

Adeline put the uniforms on the table. "I'm not going." Her voice was firm, her signing backing it up. Her hands trembled, and her eyes glistened with tears.

Agent Debone turned to her. "Yes, you are. The Herbalist killed Jasmine instead of you. He'll try again. Plus, you are the only witness who can identify the guy who shot and killed the Prime Minister."

"I know the Herbalist killed Jas instead of me. I saw it happen."

Mark did a double take. He pushed past the others. "Addie, what do you mean you saw it?"

"I've seen all of them, Mark. In a series of visions and nightmares. Guess I'm the police's star witness or something."

"For both cases and as such you need to be in a safe house." Agent Debone emphasized each word, although Nate knew that would be lost on Adeline.

"Just keep out of this a minute," Mark insisted. "Go on. Why did he kill her?"

"He killed her because he failed to kill me earlier…"

Mark shoved a hand through his hair. "What do you mean he failed earlier? When did he try to kill you? I should have let Mum cancel the cruise. They should be here."

"Mark, don't. He tried when I went to see the opening of the memorial gardens."

Mark's face darkened as he glared at the two police officers. "I thought you said—"

"Nothing's been proved yet," Agent Debone cut him off.

"I'll stay with Mark." Adeline's face paled, but remained passive.

Agent Debone shook his head. "No. I have been assigned to protect you, and I'm moving you to a safe house."

"But—"

"No buts. You don't have a choice."

Adeline glared at him and turning to Mark signed rapidly, not bothering to speak.

Nate watched fascinated. He'd learned a lot from the few lessons he'd had, but there was no way he could keep up with the speed of what she was saying, or what her brother replied. Anger flashed in her eyes, and she threw her hands up before turning her back on him.

Mark pulled her against him, holding her tightly.

"She said there was a red light shining on her. A laser sight that moved from her head down onto her chest. The Prime Minister blocked it. There were two bright flashes from across the street. Then Mrs. Williams collapsed on her as she got shot. She wants to know if the Prime Minister died in her place." Mark spoke emphatically, signing so Adeline could follow the conversation even though she had her back to him. "And so do I. Was it an assassination like the media insists, or was it a case of mistaken identity? An accident? A case of the Prime Minister stood in front of her at just the moment the gun went off?"

Nate took a deep breath, exchanging a long look with Agent Debone. "Right now, we don't know for sure. We're not going to give the media a different story to the one they're running with until we catch the guy responsible."

"Which is?"

"A deliberate assassination. But between you, me and the gatepost, CCTV shows the light from the laser on Adeline, not on the Prime Minister."

Mark inhaled sharply. He closed his eyes for a moment. "I can protect her, sure, but I can't be here all the time. I'm due on the base in half an hour as it is."

"Then let us look after her for you."

Mark sighed. "All right."

"Adeline?" Nate asked touching her arm gently.

She raised her head. Her normally bright eyes were dull and sunken. The bright countenance that usually resonated from her like a beacon had been ripped from her, replaced with dark, brooding storm clouds. "It doesn't look like I have a choice. Do I?" she asked sullenly.

"Not until we catch this guy, no. I'm sorry." Nate tried to convey his feelings in his face and signs. He hadn't realized until now just how much hearing people relied on tones of voice, not to mention tempo and volume. But with Adeline he had to rely solely on body language.

Tears glistened in her eyes. He imagined of frustration rather than grief. "So I get abandoned in some safe house, with someone I don't know, for who knows how long. A prisoner, when I have done nothing wrong."

Nate shook his head firmly. He looked at his hands, signing slowly, hoping he was getting it right.

"You're not alone. God won't abandon you." He didn't know the sign for abandon and just waved his hands.

"Abandon," Adeline showed him.

"Abandon." Nate repeated. "Neither will I. You move in with Vianne and me."

Agent Debone coughed. "Sergeant, can I have a word?"

Nate nodded. "Sure." No doubt he would get told that he couldn't do this. Well that was just tough. Fear for his and Vianne's safety aside, this was the right thing to do and he knew it.

Mark hugged Adeline. "I need to go to work. Let me know where you are."

"The whole point of a safe house, Colonel, is that no one knows where she is," Agent Debone said slowly.

Mark pulled himself up to his full height, his military bearing taking over. "Maybe secure housing on the base would be preferable." The authority on his voice was unlike anything Nate had heard before. "I can have a whole platoon of heavily armed, well trained security personnel posted outside her door, twenty-four seven. No one can get on or off the base without ID or a very good reason for being there on a good day. For the next week there will be no such thing as a good day. And if I speak to the base commander and explain why she's there, he can order a lock down, making the entire area impenetrable."

Agent Debone drew himself up to match Mark's stance. "Not an option—"

Nate moved and stood between the two men and raised his hands. "Enough already. Colonel Monroe, Mark, I promise I'll make sure Adeline's all right. Even if I can't tell you where she is, I'll make sure someone keeps you informed as to what's happening."

"All right. Thank you." Mark hugged Adeline and then signed to her.

Nate watched the conversation, picking up the odd word here or there, but nothing more. Tears ran down Adeline's face as she hugged Mark once more and then watched him leave. She rubbed her sleeve over her eyes. Then she sat at the table and picked up one of the uniform jackets.

Nate spun around so she wouldn't see what he was saying and indicated to Agent Debone to do the same. "I know what you're going to say and that's my place isn't safe or good enough. Answer me this. The Herbalist knows where she works. He also knows where she lives, and quite possibly where she goes to church on a Sunday, as well. She's just lost her best friend who also happens to be my partner's wife."

"Exactly why it's not up for debate. She goes into protective custody, whether she likes it or not. And you are not the person to do it."

Nate took a deep breath. "I'm not disputing she needs protecting. Look. School holidays start today, and I need someone to look after my niece. Move Adeline into my place. Once I'm home in the evenings I'll take over the protective detail. She can look after Vianne, give her something to do. But when I'm home, I don't want anyone else in the house."

"Sergeant, this is such a bad idea it's laughable. Have you any idea how much danger you'll be placing your niece in?"

"I've taken that into consideration. How much sign language do you speak?"

"None, but—"

"Do you have anyone who speaks sign language

in your department?" He raised an eyebrow as the agent scrunched up his nose. "I'll take that as a no. I do. Therefore she stays with me. She needs to be with people she can communicate with."

Agent Debone glared at him. "If you want tongues to wag then fine, no one else will be in the house. I've seen the way you look at her, Sergeant. I'm not saying you'd do anything inappropriate or your judgment is clouded, but you are personally involved here. I'll agree to her staying at your place on one condition. I come, too."

Nate took a deep breath.

"You know I'm right." Agent Debone's voice softened a little. "You're an elder of your church, aren't you? You know you need a third adult in the house, for both your sakes. Never mind doing things right by the child."

"All right. But you'll have to have the couch."

"The couch is fine."

****

Adeline glanced around the room as Nate put her bag on the bed. Painted a cheery yellow with yellow daisy curtains, it was nothing like she'd imagined his guest room to be. Turning to him, she signed slowly as she spoke. "A little girly for such a big macho cop, isn't it?"

Nate's body shook as he laughed. "Not my choice," he said trying to sign as well. "Vianne chose it all."

"She has good taste. Thank you for letting me stay here."

He moved over to her. "You're welcome." His

arms enfolded her in their strength and warmth, and she leaned against him. She felt his breath on her cheek and his chest rising and falling. She angled her face towards him.

"I do have rules." Was that a twinkle in his eye as he spoke?

"Do I want to know?"

"No jumping on the bed. No texting at the table. Homework is done the night you are given it." He paused, a huge grin on his face. "And, most important of all, eat your greens without complaint or there's no pudding."

She widened her eyes in mock horror. "Please, don't make me eat green stuff. I don't like green stuff."

Nate shook with laughter. "All of them," he repeated. "Then there's no TV until the homework's done, no TV on a Sunday and bed by eight-thirty."

Adeline laughed. "Enough already, or I'll regret moving in."

He leaned closer to her, his eyes softening. His left hand came up to cradle the side of her face, his right sliding across her waist. His face was inches away from hers, and her heart leapt as his lips claimed hers. She kissed him back, her eyes closing. Part of her screamed this was wrong, the other part, the part that was in control, took no notice. Her hands slid up Nate's arms, holding him.

His fingers wound through her hair as he deepened the kiss, her scalp tingling at his touch. She fitted so perfectly with him. Where did he end and she begin? Fire blazed through her, every nerve ending sparkled and lit up like bonfire night. Caught up in an avalanche of feelings, all she knew was him and the way he possessed all of her. She gave herself freely in return, not hiding anything.

He pulled back abruptly, and let go of her.

Adeline opened her eyes. Had she done something wrong? "Nate?"

"I'm sorry," he said, his cheeks turning an attractive shade of red. "I shouldn't have done that. I need to get to work. I'll see you tonight."

Before she could say anything, he left the room. Adeline touched her lips with her fingers, her throat raw and eyes stinging with raw emotion. How could he kiss her like that and just leave? And why apologize for a kiss that left her senses reeling? She turned to unpack, and caught a glimpse of Agent Debone's scowling reflection in the mirror.

9

Nate brushed past Agent Debone and walked across the hallway, his face on fire and his stomach churning. How could he have been so stupid? What if it hadn't been Agent Debone coughing in the doorway? What if Vianne had been around and wandered in? What sort of example would he be setting? Having Adeline stay here might not be such a good idea.

"I shouldn't need to say it." Agent Debone pointed out as they reached the top of the stairs. "Because you know about inappropriate behavior and getting involved, as we had that conversation an hour or so ago, and you told me it wasn't going to happen."

Nate had no excuse, and wasn't going to offer one. "I'm sorry."

"Sorry you kissed her or sorry you got caught?"

Nate's face burned harder, knowing full well he was sorry he got caught. But admitting that wasn't something he really wanted to do.

Debone sighed, not waiting for an answer. "Once we catch this guy, and we *will* catch him, then feel free to pursue a relationship with Miss Monroe. Promise me it won't happen again, and we'll say no more about it. Otherwise she and I are out of here, and I report you to your commanding officer."

He'd had that conversation with the DI, too. He may very well find himself busted down to constable and back on the streets in uniform. Probably directing traffic. "Thanks."

"Good." Agent Debone lowered his voice. "Since your partner's wife died, neither of you are thinking straight."

Nate held his gaze, tempted to tell him he'd liked Adeline since he first met her in the doll hospital, before she got involved in this case. "I know that. I have to go or I'm going to be late. If Adeline remembers any more, or has another vision, call me immediately."

"Of course. That goes without saying."

"Thanks. School finishes at lunchtime today. Cassie will pick Vianne up at one-fifteen, and take her back to the manse to play with Lara. I'll collect her from there and be home around six." Nate grabbed his keys and headed out into the blazing sunshine, his face still hot.

Birds sang in the trees lining the street as he got in the car. He slammed the door, and shoved the keys into the ignition. Propping his elbows on the steering wheel, he buried his head in his hands, praying hard. He liked Adeline. If he were honest he liked her far too much. Once this was over he had every intention of pursing her, courting her, dating her, whatever the current word was. But until then he had to remain professional. But he couldn't do that. Not without a lot of help from the Lord.

He drove to work, arriving with no clear idea how he got there. His desk was a mess and moving a pile of papers to make a space didn't really make an impact. He slumped into his chair and glanced at Dane's empty desk next to his. A wooden framed photo of Dane, with his arms wrapped around Jas, the sun setting behind them, sat on it, their smiles taunting him. They should have had years left together, watching the kids grow, and playing with their grandchildren. Instead it was over. Jodie and Vicky were motherless, and Dane was a widower.

Nate closed his eyes, incoherent, wordless prayers falling from him. Footsteps jerked him out of his thoughts, a second before a hand dropped on his shoulder. He glanced up into a concerned face. "Hey, Guv."

DI Welsh half smiled, a yellow folder clasped in her free hand. "How are you doing, Nate?"

He shrugged.

"Are you sure you should be here?"

"Where else should I be?" Nate nodded to the papers on his desk. "It'll take a month of Sundays just to go through this lot. I'm also waiting for the coroner to ring. I'm going to attend the post mortem."

"Is that a good idea?"

He resisted the urge to snap. Attending Jasmine's autopsy wasn't going to be a picnic, he knew that. But he needed to go. "It's something I have to do."

"All right." DI Welsh paused, staring at him intently. "I hear Miss Monroe is staying at your place."

How did she find out so fast? Silly question. Debone must have told her.

"Yeah. As is Agent Debone from MI5."

She perched on the edge of his desk, resting the yellow folder on her lap. "Is that a sensible idea? Even if we set aside our conversation last night, you're an elder in your church. You also have a small, impressionable child in the house. Besides which there is a killer out there after her."

"I know what I'm doing."

"I'm inclined to disagree with that. By putting Miss Monroe in your house, you're putting yourself and your niece in danger."

"Look, Guv. I'm there all evening and all night. Agent Debone is there the whole time." Nate pushed a hand through his hair. "Where else do I put her?" he snapped. "If MI5 hide her away, we lose the only advantage we have. The guy they assigned to her is a complete idiot, not to mention rude and ill mannered. He actually turned his back on Adeline to discuss her with her brother. He told her he wasn't talking to her, so it didn't matter if she couldn't see his lips move."

DI Welsh straightened and tapped the folder on her thigh. "That's way beyond being rude. He should know better."

"Tell me about it. She saw her best friend killed yesterday, never mind having the Prime Minister die in her arms. Agent Debone's adamant it doesn't concern her. Adeline needs to be around friends right now, not some..." He broke off, not wanting to say something he'd regret. Or say something that put him into the same rude category he'd just placed Agent Debone.

DI Welsh nodded. "Just be careful."

"I am. Agent Debone is sleeping downstairs so we have the whole house covered. Hopefully, we can clear this up in a few days, and everything can go back to normal. Well, as normal as possible for Dane and the kids."

The phone rang and Nate reached to answer it. "DS Holmes...Thanks, I'll be right there. Don't start without me." He hung up. "They're ready to do the post mortem."

"That can wait five minutes. You might want to

take a look at this first. Lots of pictures of our pony-tailed friend." She held out the file. "It's the best the tech guys could do. We're running them through the database now, but so far nothing."

"Thanks." He put the file on his desk.

"Look at it, Nate. The post mortem can wait a few minutes."

Nate tried not to sigh as he picked up the file. He opened it, flicking through the images. "It's the same guy. Nice shades. No shades. Dark tee shirt, dark slacks." He paused. "Why so many shots?"

"They're taken from various CCTV cameras over the past few weeks—one from each road the victim was found on. Along with the one from the doll hospital."

Nate kept his gaze on the man in the picture, burning the image into his mind. "I'll deal with this when I get back. I don't want to hold them up." He wrote a cryptic note and stuck it onto the file. "Thanks for this."

DI Welsh stood. "Welcome. See you later."

****

Adeline checked the door. There was no one there. She shook her head and glanced back at the mirror. The reflection had gone, no doubt chasing after Nate. Had Agent Debone watched them kiss, was that why Nate pulled away so fast? Or was it simply because he realized what he was doing—kissing her in his house and in a bedroom?

One thing she did know. She had to keep tight rein on the gradually increasing deep feelings she had for Nate. He was a church elder and a police officer. He had to be above reproach. They both did. She put her coat on and grabbed her bag and the leash. "Come on then, Ben, let's go. We're late as it is."

She clipped the leash onto Ben's collar and headed to the door.

Agent Debone stood in front of it. His eyes glittered, and his mood looked darker than normal.

"Where are you going?" He folded arms over his chest, blocking her path.

"Work."

"No way."

"Yes, way."

"I don't think so."

"Why not?"

"Because there's a man out there who wants you dead." He leaned closer, his eyes narrowing, and his face turning red.

Adeline raised her eyebrow. "Shouting at me won't make me hear you any better."

"How do you know I'm shouting? You're deaf." His arms waved at her, and he was well and truly in her personal space.

Adeline signed at him, her own movements jerky and over exaggerated. "Your body language gives you away. You are right in my face. And you say I'm deaf like it's a disease. Well it's not. It's who I am. I just happen to speak a different language than you. Or do you treat French or Polish people the same way?"

He backed off a pace. "You're not going out."

"I have to work. I have deadlines to meet, along with a whole load of toys that need returning and mending today. I can't let down the children."

"This perp knows where you are." He leaned against the door.

"Good. Let him come."

"Don't be stupid."

His attitude was enough to make her want to hit her head against a brick wall. "Don't talk to me as if I'm a child. I have God, Ben, and Nate looking after me. And you."

"Do you and DS Holmes have to bring God into everything?"

"Of course. Why? Don't you?"

"God is for..." He turned around, cutting off the rest of his words as she couldn't read his lips.

Adeline sighed. He knew how infuriating that was. He did it deliberately.

"Well, I have no idea what he said, Ben, but I can make a good guess. God is for church, Sundays and religious nuts. Guess that makes me a fruitcake. Good job I like them."

She ruffled his ears and glanced up to see the scowl on Agent Debone's face deepen as he turned back. As much as she didn't want this, it was imperative she at least tried to get on with him

"Ben needs a walk, and I need to go in and check the current workload. You can come with me. Sit in the corner or whatever it is you do all day. I'm really not trying to be difficult. I just want to do my job, the same as you."

"Then we drive."

"Ben needs a walk."

"I'll take him around the block or let him out in the garden."

Adeline reached into her pocket and pulled out a plastic bag. "Then you'll need this."

"Miss Monroe—"

"Agent Debone. It's called being a responsible dog

owner. All he'll need is ten minutes twice a day."

"I'll have someone take him once you get into work. We'll take my car. It's raining."

"I'd rather walk. I have a coat, an umbrella. What more do I need?"

"A lift. Until further notice we do things my way or we don't do them at all."

She resisted the urge to salute. "Fine. A lift it is."

****

Nate's paper covered shoes whispered against the tiled floor as he entered the morgue.

"It's nice of you to finally join us, Sergeant." Professor Jacobs, the home office pathologist's curt tone cut the air as sharply as any scalpel he might wield. Several blue suited figures in identical surgical garb to the one Nate currently wore stood around the autopsy table. "We were waiting for you. We have a lot of work to do this morning."

Nate's jaw clenched and he dug his gloved nails into his palms. He was irritated enough as it was without smart aleck pathologists making it worse. "We all have a lot work to do. What doesn't help is being caught by the boss as I was about to leave."

"Sounds fun."

"She gave me a shed load more files to add to the mounting pile on my desk." Nate glanced around the room, starting slightly at the one person he wasn't expecting to see. "Dane? What are you doing here? The Guv would have a blue fit and go up in smoke if she knew."

Dane jerked his head in the direction of Professor Jacobs. "He's already done that. I have to be here."

"No, you don't." Nate spoke gently.

"I need to know who killed my wife."

"We know who it was. She had the herbs in her pocket."

Dane's voice shook. "Even so, I—"

Nate put a hand on Dane's arm, moving between him and the table where Jasmine's covered body lay. "Dane, mate, this isn't just another body or another victim lying there. It's *your wife*." He enunciated every word. "The woman you've lived with and loved for the last twenty years. You know her like the back of your hand. Do you really want your last memory of her to be like this?"

His eyes searched those of his friend intently. "You know what a post mortem entails. What we need to do to her body."

"I owe it to her to be here." Dane's eyes glistened and his voice cracked. "I owe it to her and to the girls not to leave."

"No, mate. You owe it to her to remember how she was. Let me do this for the both of you. Come on." Nate gently led Dane to the door.

Professor Jacobs glanced up. "You can wait in my office, Dane. I should have the preliminary results when we're done."

Dane nodded, his eyes haunted.

Nate kept up the pressure until Dane finally agreed to wait in the office. He closed the door behind him, and then went back over to the table as the autopsy started.

****

Still angry over the amount of effort it had taken to

get here, Adeline got out of the car without waiting for Agent Debone to turn off the engine. His whole attitude toward her was demeaning. She wasn't a crackpot or an idiot. It was people like him who'd prevented her from coming forward in the first place.

Stamping her way across the pavement, she unlocked the door to the doll hospital and deactivated the alarm. She let Ben off the leash and shook her head. No surprise there. Susie hadn't opened up—she was late. Again.

Agent Debone caught hold of her arm, stopping her in the doorway. "I need to check the place. Make sure it's safe."

Adeline sighed and pulled her collar up against the cold and damp. "The alarm was on, and the building was locked, but sure, feel free. I'll stand right here. In the rain, getting wet."

Debone nodded. "While I go inside, in the dry, to ensure there is no one here that shouldn't be." He grimaced. "I'm just doing my job."

She watched him go. "And I'm just trying to do mine." *Because if I sit around and do nothing but think about what's happened I'll go insane. Or cry. And neither is an option.* Ben wagged his tail, spraying water over her legs. She shook her head. "Did that on purpose, didn't you, you daft dog," she said, a wry smile on her face.

Ben rubbed his head against her and plopped down at her feet. She waited until she got the all clear then headed over to reception to check the messages.

Susie ran in from the rain, dripping water from her umbrella onto the floor. She pulled off her raincoat and hung it on the coat rack in the corner. Her long hair had beads braided into the end of each plait, with a head band around her forehead. A bright floor-length gaudy skirt and waistcoat over her pillar-box red blouse completed the ensemble. She spoke around the gum in her mouth. "I'm so sorry I'm late, Dr. A. My bus didn't turn up, like, so I had to walk."

"It's fine. I've only just got here myself."

"I wasn't sure you'd be coming with Jasmine, like, dying and everything. It's terrible. Do you think they'll catch who did it?"

"Of course they will. Susie, this is—" She broke off realizing she didn't know his first name.

Agent Debone extended a hand to Susie. "Debone, Agent Gladstone Debone."

"Well, pleased to meet you, Debone, Agent Gladstone Debone. I'm Susie Vickers. I man the front desk. How do you know Dr. A? Are you her boyfriend? Because I thought she was seeing that cop." Susie shook his hand, speaking quickly.

Adeline shook her head. "I'm not seeing Nate. And I only met Agent Debone yesterday."

"Speaking of yesterday. It was so cool seeing you on the TV like that. It must have been so neat meeting the Prime Minister. Not neat having her die on you, like, but being the last person to talk to her. That's like deep, really deep."

"Deep?" Adeline ran her gaze over Susie's attire. "You've been spending too much time with that new hippy fellow of yours. What's his name?"

"Storm. Isn't that cool?" A soppy, wistful expression crossed Susie's face. "I think I should change my name. I fancy Rainbow. Goes well with Storm."

"His mother named him Storm?"

Susie beamed and started setting up the desk. "Yeah. He was born during, like, a really bad thunderstorm. He's kind, chatty, loves kids and animals. He has these, like, really intense eyes and—"

"Susie," Adeline interrupted her. "Do me a favor."

"What's that?"

"Stop saying like and really. And put the gum in the bin."

"But I've been, like—"

Adeline held up a hand. "It's unprofessional." *Not to mention extremely irritating.*

"Sure thing, Dr. A."

Adeline headed into the back room to begin work. Ben settled at her feet, and Agent Debone sat opposite her.

She spent ten minutes gluing the pieces of a broken doll back together. She glanced across the room. "Agent Debone, are you just going to sit there all day?"

"Pretty much."

"And when I need the bathroom? Are you going to sit outside the door, too?"

"Pretty much."

"Is that all you can say?"

There was a long pause.

Agent Debone rested a finger on his chin. "Pretty much." He sat impassively for a moment and then smiled.

Adeline shook her head with a grin and pulled a drawer open. She flipped through the top file. Jasmine's neat handwriting covered the page. Unexpected emotion flooded and eyes burning, she ran for the small bathroom, locking the door.

10

Time slowed to a point where Adeline didn't know anything but grief. She poured her heart out in prayer. Fervent, wordless cries rose from the depths of her soul, to the feet of the One whom she knew understood even though she couldn't voice them.

Ben nudged her.

She rubbed the top of his head. "What is it?"

He ran to the door and hit it with a paw.

Reluctantly Adeline moved to the bathroom door. She opened it to find Nate standing there holding a takeout cup. "Oh…"

Adeline dragged her sleeve over her face. She must look a sight. "Hi…"

"We were passing and thought you'd like this." He offered the cup.

She slid into the hallway and shut the door behind her. "Thank you." Taking it from him, the scent of chocolate and steam hit her, like a breath of fresh air. The sheer comfort factor of chocolate was already working its magic.

"It has cream and marshmallows in it."

"Just the way I like it. Thank you."

"I owe you an apology."

Adeline looked at him. For the life of her she couldn't think what he had to apologize for. "No, you don't."

"Yes, I do. For kissing you before I went to work."

"Oh." Shaking hands almost dropped the chocolate. "You don't need to apologize. It was as much me as it was you."

"I'm not apologizing for kissing you, you silly girl. I'm apologizing for breaking off as abruptly as I did and then walking out on you. The only reason I did, was because we were being watched."

"Agent Debone. I caught a glimpse of him in the mirror after you left."

"Yes. And my spare bedroom isn't really the place for that kind of affection. I have to take Vianne into consideration." He let out a deep breath. "Besides, I'm only human. If I keep kissing you like that, I might not be able to stop, and I can't allow that to happen, for either of our sakes. I like you, Adeline. I like you a lot."

"I like you, too." *More than like you.*

Something in his eyes flickered. She could so easily get swallowed in the depths of his gaze. She wanted to dive into the safety of his arms and never come out. To lean her head against his firm chest as it rose and fell with his breath, and feel his heart beating. His hand gently brushed tears from her cheeks. Electricity sparked from his fingers sending warmth flooding through her body. She shook herself mentally. It couldn't happen.

"You said *we* were passing?"

"Yeah. Dane's here, too. He wanted to come in to see you. He said something about clearing Jas's desk, but I don't know if he's up to that yet."

"There's no rush on that. Her stuff isn't going anywhere."

They walked into her office where Dane stood by her desk.

She set the cup on the side of the desk and

wrapped her arms tightly around him. "I'm really sorry. I loved her so much."

Huge sobs welled up from within him as he hugged her back. "Me, too. I can't believe she's not coming home."

She stood there, holding him tightly, then guided him to a chair by her desk. "There's no rush on Jas's things. They can stay here until you're ready."

"Thanks."

Adeline glanced up as a tray set down on her desk. Susie had brought in a flask of tea, papers tucked under her arm.

"Thanks Susie."

"No problem, Dr. A. There are three visitors in the main ward. There's, like, one discharge for you to sign, and one admission. I've, like, done all the paperwork." She put the papers on the desk and held out a pen. "I said the repairs would, like, take about a week, and you'd call if they'd be any different. They were fine once I explained we were short staffed right now."

"Thanks." Adeline signed the papers and handed them back.

"Is it all right if I leave early, like? I know I was late, but I, like, have a date and—"

Adeline held up a hand. Unable to put off a certain conversation any longer, she wasn't about to have it in front of the others. Not only would that show a lack of respect and leadership, Dane didn't need any of Susie's off-hand comments. "Susie, let's step into the hall for a moment."

She glanced at the three men. "Excuse us. I'll be right outside, not going anywhere."

Adeline closed the office door for a bit of privacy then turned to address her wayward employee. "You'll have to make up time tomorrow, or I'll dock your wages. As you pointed out, we are shorthanded as it is right now, without you coming and going as you please. You've been late in and late back from every break for the past two or three weeks. That's if you come in at all."

"Sorry, but, like, you know how it is—"

"No, actually I don't."

Jasmine was dead and Susie wanted time off—for a date? She pushed a hand through her hair and fiddled with the cross around her neck. Perhaps Susie's need to leave was no different than her insisting on coming into work. Just a different way of dealing with things.

"Yeah all right, Susie. Ring for the end of visiting in fifteen minutes and then go. Lock up on your way out. Have fun on your date. Just be on time tomorrow. Otherwise, it'll go down in your file as a warning."

Susie nodded, not losing the glazed expression or looking in the least bit repentant, and headed down the hallway.

Adeline returned to the office. She sat and picked up her drink in trembling hands. She took a small sip then slammed her cup down, spilling cocoa across the papers spread over her desk.

****

Nate's hands clenched and unclenched as he watched Adeline struggle for composure. He found it incredibly hard being a silent witness to her distress. He wanted to hold and comfort her, take her in his arms, kiss her, and assure her that everything would be all right, but Agent Debone's presence forbade it. As did his common sense.

Lord, give her the comfort I am unable to. Help me keep my sense of propriety around her, until such a time that I can openly show my feelings for her. Let us find the Herbalist soon, before any more lives are lost.

Everyone sat squashed in Adeline's office. Big enough for one, it was not designed to seat four.

Nate put a hand on her clenched fist. He rubbed it gently, his other hand pulling out a handkerchief to mop up with. "Adeline—"

"Sorry."

Adeline buried her head in her hands. Nate rubbed her back, ignoring the black looks Agent Debone shot him. She needed the comfort, and he would give it. He squeezed her hand as Dane started to speak, smiling as he noticed Ben nudge her at the same time.

"I want to go over everything you know about the Herbalist. Every dream, case, vision, every detail. Maybe we missed something, or there's something you didn't remember before. Something that could help us catch him."

Agent Debone glared at him. "You're off the case. Shouldn't you be at home with your kids? Or did you send them to school for the last day of term?"

"Jodie insisted on going to school. Her class is having a teddy bears picnic and Jas had made cakes for her to take in. My parents have taken Vicky out somewhere with them—probably to the park. Jas's parents have gone to the undertaker and manse. I have nothing else to do, except sit in an empty house and remember what I've lost. Let me help find her killer. I'll beg if I have to."

Nate exchanged a long look with Agent Debone.

Dane needed this.

Nate nodded. "No need to beg though, mate. You can take notes. Might keep your mind focused. And if the Guv asks, you were never here."

"That's not a problem. I'm not going to jeopardize this case in any way." Dane pulled out his notebook. "Now you said the Herbalist was protecting them from something or someone in every case."

Nate held up a hand. "Just take notes, mate. Let us ask the questions." He glanced at Adeline. "What he asked."

"Yeah. He'd tell them as he strangled them that this was for their own good, and that they'd be safe now. Sometimes he'd say they deserved it."

"Did you see all eight of the murders?" Agent Debone asked.

"Yes."

"And you didn't go to the police sooner? Why not?"

Nate didn't like the agent's tone of voice but Adeline didn't hear the snide inflection and he was not about to point it out.

Adeline answered the question. "I didn't think they'd believe me. I mean, look what kind of press psychics get. They get laughed at and slammed for being too late. I've never had visions or anything like this before. I had no idea what was happening. So, I put it down to coincidence, too much cheese before bed or a bad curry, but after a few more and they were so accurate, I knew what I had to do and spoke to Nate."

"You did the right thing," Nate said. "And *we* believed you. You knew things we hadn't released to the press. Dane and I knew there was no way you were faking it."

Getting up, he crossed over to the whiteboard with

the list of patients and picked up the cloth. "May I?" As Adeline nodded, he cleaned the board and began writing. "OK, we have parsley, ragwort, onion, tamarisk, euphorbia, clover, toadflax, and ivy."

Dane pulled his reading glasses off and chewed the ends. "There's no connection. It doesn't even make a pattern on a map."

"And it's no recipe I've ever come across," Agent Debone added. "The wife's a chef so I know a fair few."

Nate studied the words. Suddenly the penny dropped, and it made perfect sense. He wiped the board and rewrote them in a bullet list. He circled the first letter of each word, joining them together as if he were playing a word search. "Yes, there is. We have P. R. O. T. E. C. T. I. It could be protective, but if I were a betting man, I would put next month's pay on the fact he's spelling protection. I have no idea what the herbs mean, but I can make an educated guess."

"Protection," they all chorused.

Nate couldn't understand why he hadn't seen it sooner. "That leaves O and N. Does anyone have a map?"

"At home," Adeline said. "I don't need one here."

"I have one in the car. I'll go get it." Agent Debone hurried from the room.

Dane raised his gaze heavenward. "But why kill Jas? What was he protecting her from? I never laid a hand on her, or the girls."

Adeline wrung her hands together. A haunted look filled her eyes, and she shrank in her seat. Her pale skin was almost translucent, and if Nate put any stock in the 'looks like she's seen a ghost' line, that's how he'd describe her.

"He's after me," she managed. "Because I know who he is. He was in my house waiting for me and killed her by mistake. That's why I'm in protective custody, isn't it?"

Nate sat on the corner of the desk and put a hand on her shoulder. "Officially, it's because you know who killed the Prime Minister, but unofficially, yeah. That is the way we're looking at this now."

"It's my fault Jas died, just like it's my fault the Prime Minister died. I shouldn't have said anything about the visions. I shouldn't have gone out. I don't deserve you protecting me. I should just let him finish the job. Then these people wouldn't have died for me."

Grabbing her face, Nate gently held it in place so she didn't miss anything he said. "No. Don't ever say that or wish yourself dead." He let go, copying her signs as he spoke. "It's not your fault. No one asked Jas to be in your house last night. I don't know why she had to die. I don't suppose even Pastor Jack could tell us that. Only God knows why this happened. I know this is hard on all of us, but we have to find this bloke and see justice done. For Jas and all the others."

He shot Dane a quick glance. "And I'm sure Dane doesn't blame you, either."

Adeline turned to face Dane.

"No I don't," he managed. "I wish God hadn't taken her, but it's not your fault. Pastor Jack came over last night. He said, he said that as much as the girls and I needed Jas, that she had finished her task here on Earth and that God had more need of her. You…" his voice shook, but he didn't drop his gaze. "…are, and always will be, a dear friend. It wasn't your fault. You didn't kill her."

"OK," she whispered.

"Why are these things always in the last place you look?" Agent Debone came back with the map. "There is one road named for a plant starting with *N* and four with *O*. I have no idea what they mean, but we have oak, orange, orchid, olive and nettle. Nettle is a given as that's the only *N*."

Adeline took a deep breath. "We'll need an internet connection or medicinal plant or symbolism book. I don't have either here. The internet is too much of a temptation for Susie to spend all day on social networking sites."

"You could just block them like they have at work." Nate winked at her. "Dane was always on there, uploading photos or checking the latest celebrity gossip."

His partner shot him a half smile. "That's a tad less destructive than eating at the desk and dropping crumbs and half a mug of coffee on the keyboard."

"Only ever did it on your keyboard. I'll ring the Guv. We'll need to put unmarked cars on all those roads around the clock." He pulled out his phone and dialed. "Guv it's Nate. Can you do a search on herb meanings for me? Adeline has no 'net." He rolled his eyes at Dane and mimed winding a handle to speed things up. "Unless you want to waste manpower by staking out five roads when you don't need to? Yes, we worked out the link and know what the Herbalist is doing. We need definitions for the following roads. Oak, orange, orchid, and olive. We're looking for ones meaning protection, that's what he's spelling out."

Pacing over to the white board, he wiped out the ones they didn't need. "Right. So those two and nettle. Yeah, Adeline's right here. Why?" His stomach twisted and skin crawled. Never mind any other form of protection, right now they needed the Lord's protection.

He turned around and faced the window. "Are you sure?" he barked into the phone. His mind whirled. That possibility hadn't occurred to him. Was it just coincidence or was there some darker force at work here? Whatever it was, it worried him deeply.

"OK, will do. Yes, a car outside my place and here as well is a sensible precaution. And before you suggest it, no we're not going to find a new safe house." He listened for a moment, and then let out a deep breath. "Fine. If that's what you want. Yeah, see you later." He closed the phone and slid it into his jacket pocket.

Dane studied the board. "Oak and olive?"

He spun around and nodded. "Yeah, both mean protection, amongst other things. The guv is putting a watch on all three of them until further notice. Adeline, who named this place Datura?"

"Dad did when he founded it. I kept the name when I bought this place and moved the doll hospital here. Why?"

"Datura is an herb. Did you know?"

"Yeah. The doll hospital was originally on Datura Drive, hence its name. Why? What does it mean?"

"Datura, like all the rest of these plants, means several things. But one of the meanings is protection." He took in the shock on the faces around him. "So as well as having Agent Debone or myself around all the time, there will be a car out at the front of the building. You're also going back to my place, right now. No argument. I'm going to ring Cassie and get her to bring Vianne home. Would you mind keeping an eye on her until I get back?"

Agent Debone looked at him. "My car's outside. Tell me where to go and I'll collect Vianne on the way back to your place."

"Thank you. She's at the manse. Adeline knows where that is. I'll let Cassie know you're coming."

****

Adeline stood at the sink in Nate's kitchen, peeling potatoes and carrots for dinner. She was actually looking forward to the baby-sitting.

Vianne wasn't a bother and was old enough to get on with stuff without help. Take now, for example. Vianne sat at the table going through the pack of crazy bands she had bought on the way home from school.

Agent Debone sat reading the paper. He seemed the type of man who expected meals to appear and dishes to clean themselves, before neatly piling themselves back in the cupboard again.

Ben nudged Adeline's leg, and she glanced down at him before looking over at the table.

Vianne smiled at her. "How long are you staying here for?"

"I don't know. Just a few days I hope. It depends when the police say I can have my house back."

"OK." She tugged the dappy hat down further over her ears and looked at Agent Debone. "Is there something wrong with your house, too?"

"Something wrong with my house?"

"Yeah."

"Why?" He put the paper down and tilted his head at her.

"Cos you're living here, too." She pointed to his ring. "Did you have a fight with your wife?"

"Oh. Nothing's wrong, just staying here for a few days."

"Why?"

"Because Miss Monroe is staying here."

"You're not her boyfriend because you're married, so it must be something else. Why?"

"Because your daddy asked me to stay."

"I don't have a daddy. This is Uncle Nate's house. Why did he ask you?"

Agent Debone heaved a huge sigh, his shoulders shaking. "You ask too many questions."

"That's because I'm a cop's niece."

Adeline laughed as much at Vianne's response as the look of outrage on the MI5 agent's face. "That you are. Who told you that?"

"Miss Pringle at school. She says I'd make a good cop 'cos I never know when to shut up."

"That's not a very nice thing to say." Agent Debone turned back to his paper.

Vianne tugged at her hat again. "She hates me. They all do."

"I'm sure they don't hate you." Adeline added the potatoes to the pan of water.

"Yes, they do."

Adeline tilted her head. "Why's that?"

"'Cos I'm weird." Vianne flicked the pile of bands across the table.

Adeline put the knife down and sat next to her. "Who says that?"

"They all do."

"Just the kids?" Adeline helped pick up all the bands.

"Not just them, the teachers, too. It's because of my hats. They say I have no right to be there. That I should be in a special school for weird kids."

"I used to be called weird too, because I wasn't like them. I couldn't hear, therefore couldn't do music and movement, or sing or play with them in the playground. But I happen to like your hats. Especially this one, it's bright yellow, and that's my favorite color. It's quirky."

Vianne tilted her head at her. "What's that mean?"

"It means original or individual. Something special only to you."

"So, a good thing?"

"Yes, Vianne." Adeline smiled. "A very good thing. Tell me something. Does Jodie think you're weird?"

"No. She's my friend. She was sad today 'cos her mummy died." Vianne started crying. "I didn't know what to say to make her feel better."

Adeline hugged her. "Sometimes you don't need to say anything. Just being there or giving her a hug will do. She's going to need her friends. Especially one like you."

"Is that 'cos I don't have a mummy, either?"

"Yes, you know how she's feeling."

"I can show her that people still love her and that it's OK to cry. Plus she still has her daddy and her sister."

"And you have Uncle Nate."

"Who do you have?" Vianne gazed at Adeline intently.

"I have my brother. He's in the army. And my mum and dad. They're on holiday on a big cruise ship at the moment." She straightened Vianne's hat. "Why do you wear the hats?"

"The hat keeps me safe."

"Doesn't Uncle Nate keep you safe?"

Vianne pulled the hat crooked again. "Yeah, I guess so."

"But...?" Adeline grinned at her.

"He's not always here. He works a lot."

"He's a policeman. He works to keep you safe."

Vianne sighed. "He gets hurt sometimes. Like his nose or he gets bruises. He got shot once in the arm. Then he was in hospital and I had to go stay with Nanny. That was no fun."

Adeline thought for a moment, praying for the right words. "Being a policeman can be dangerous, but you know what? Jesus looks after him while he's at work. All the time. Keeps him safe and if something really bad did happen, Jesus would be right there with him. Just like He was with Auntie Jas. So being scared is OK because we're never alone."

"That's good. I love Uncle Nate lots."

"He loves you lots, too."

"Like Jesus does?"

"Just like that. And because Uncle Nate has to work over the summer holidays he's asked me to look after you. So if you like, you can come to work with me during the week. Help take care of the dolls."

"Can I be Nurse Vianne? And have a uniform and everything?"

"That is a brilliant idea. How about we text Uncle Nate and ask him to pick one up on his way home? The party store in the precinct should have one. Can you pass me the phone?"

Vianne beamed and passed over the phone. "Cool."

Adeline texted Nate. Not a normal phone, all she could do on this was text. But it would do as a temporary replacement. "Now we need to finish dinner, or it won't be ready."

"Is *he* coming to the doll hospital, too?"

"Agent Debone? Yes, he is."

Vianne scrunched up her nose in thought. "What's he going to be? Because if you're the doctor and I'm the nurse, he needs a job, too."

Adeline looked at Agent Debone. "He does. That's a very good question. What job could we give him?"

He kept a straight face. "I'm going to be the chair leg."

Vianne laughed, holding her sides, her face wide with delight. "That's silly."

Agent Debone did his best not to smile. "I always said I'd be a chair leg when I grew up. This is my chance."

"People can't be chair legs. You could be the man who pushes the patients to x-ray." Vianne giggled.

"A porter?" The horrified expression on his face was priceless.

Adeline wished she had a camera.

"Yeah." Vianne agreed. "A porter."

Adeline laughed. "Sounds good to me."

He folded his arms and frowned. "Wait till they hear about this back at the office. I'd rather be a chair leg."

11

Nate sat on the bed next to Vianne as she finished saying her prayers. Leaning forward, he kissed her forehead. "Night, pumpkin. See you in the morning."

He was almost at the door when she spoke again. "Uncle Nate, are you going to die like Auntie Jasmine did?"

Shock resonated though him. He sat beside her. "No, honey, nothing is going to happen to me."

"But you can't be sure of that. You chase bad guys every day. One of them may have a gun or a knife or you could get in a car crash when you go really fast."

He pulled her to sit on his knees and wrapped his arms around her. "I promise to be careful. God willing, nothing is going to happen to me for a very, very long time." He moved a hand though her hair as she clung to him, not saying anything. "What happened to Auntie Jasmine was horrible. But it doesn't mean it'll happen to me."

"It happened to Mummy and Daddy. And they were on a plane and meant to be safe."

Nate closed his eyes tightly. "Yes, it did." He struggled to find the words to comfort her. *Even though I still miss Pete, and Jas died in such a horrible way. Lord, help me explain to her so that she'll understand.*

Calmness and peace filled his spirit and he opened his eyes. "You remember the story in the Bible about the sparrows and how God loves them and that He knows every single one of them by name?"

She nodded. "Yes."

"Well, He loves us way, way more than the sparrows. He knows how many days He wants you to live here on Earth, before He calls you home to heaven to live with Him. I don't know when that will be for you or for me, but it won't happen a minute before God wants it."

"Even in a bad way?" Vianne whispered.

He hugged her securely. "We can't choose how we die, but in that instant, we're not alone. And the second it happens, we're with Jesus in heaven. I miss your Daddy, but I know he's home, and I'll see him again one day. He's just living in a different country now."

"Like Australia? That's a long, long way away and they have to live upside down. Do they even have electricity there?"

Nate's grin turned into a chuckle. "Yes, they have electricity in Australia. They don't need it in heaven, though."

"Nope, 'cos Jesus is there. Are you scared cos the bad man's still out there?"

"Maybe a little."

Her wide blue eyes stared up at him. "It's OK to be scared a little. Adeline said so, cos you have Jesus right next to you."

"Yeah, we do. And that's a good thing."

Vianne hugged him tightly. "A very good thing. And He'll love us and look after us, right?"

"Right. You all right to sleep now?" She nodded, and he kissed her forehead. "In that case, good night. Sleep tight. Don't let the bed bugs bite. And if they do…"

"Squish 'em," Vianne shrieked with delight. She

leapt off his lap and snuggled down under the covers.

Ten minutes later, Nate carried a tray of coffee into the lounge.

A soap opera played on the TV in the corner, the closed captions at the bottom of the screen. Despite that, the volume was louder than he'd normally have it. *Probably Agent Debone making a point.* He set the tray down and grabbed the remote, hitting the volume minus button a couple of times.

"Here's the coffee I promised about half an hour ago." He handed one to Adeline and another to Agent Debone. "I hear Vianne is restaffing the doll hospital for you."

"Thank you. Yes, she is. She's the nurse, and Agent Debone here is the porter."

"I tried chair leg, but she wasn't having any of it. I'm never going to live porter down in the office."

Nate laughed. "Chair leg might be a bit harder to write in the report."

"True. But *porter*?"

"It could be worse. She could have made you tea lady and told you to wear a maid's uniform."

The agent choked and sprayed coffee down his shirt.

Nate pulled a handful of tissues from the box on the coffee table and handed them to him. "Are you OK?"

Agent Debone nodded his thanks and set the cup down, mopping up.

Adeline sipped her coffee. "Did she tell you that she also wants me to put one of those barrels onto Ben's collar in case the dolls get thirsty? I guess we should be grateful she thinks they carry juice and doesn't realize it's whiskey."

Nate grinned. "He's a King Charles Spaniel, not a Saint Bernard."

"Try telling Vianne that. As far as she is concerned, a dog is a dog. They come in two sizes, big and little. But just like a woman can do a man's job, so a little dog can do the same job as a big dog. Her words not mine."

Ben sighed, his head on his paws, one ear alert, the other folded down. His tail thumped gently against Adeline's leg.

She reached down to pet him. "You've taught Vianne equality for women almost too well, Nate."

Nate's shoulders raised in a shrug. "I don't want her growing up thinking she can paint herself like a doll, bat her eyelids, and play men for what she can get. A woman is an equal partner, not a possession. Same goes for a bloke."

"Are you saying that you don't believe in protecting someone you love?"

Rivers of energy poured through his already taut body, tightening it like a bow string. If only they were alone just for a few minutes so he could show her how he felt about her.

"I'm not saying that at all. To protect someone I love, I would carry her over puddles, give her my coat in a rain storm, open and close doors, give up my seat on the bus or train. Then there's making cocoa, the occasional dinner…" He answered her grin with one of his own. "And lay down my life for them if that's what the situation calls for."

"*Them*? Just how many women are you in love with, Nate?"

Nate glanced down at his cup. *Stupid… how do I get out of this one?*

"Well?" She wasn't going to let it drop.

"Well, there's Mum, my cousin Judy, Vianne." He held her gaze and switched to sign language to finish, "and you. You have no idea how much I love you."

Her smile lit her eyes and melted his heart even further. "Love you, too," she signed back.

A cough from across the room reminded him they weren't alone and that Agent Debone didn't understand what they were saying.

Nate raised his cup towards his mouth then paused midair. "Though Vianne might be a little miffed to discover she's only third on the list." He returned to speech.

"Better third than not on the list altogether," Adeline teased. "But we won't tell her."

"Good, because if she found out, she'd probably make me the man who scrubbed the floors with a toothbrush, or cleaned the toilets, or something equally nasty at the doll hospital. Or tea lady."

"Don't give her ideas," Agent Debone chimed in. "She may change my job to any one of those when she realizes I'm not going anywhere. I've been told to protect her as well."

Nate swung around sharply, coffee threatening to spill onto his lap. "*What?*"

"Just a precaution, nothing more."

He struggled to get the words past the lump in his throat. "Are you saying Vianne's in danger?"

"Nothing of the kind. You know what the powers that be are like."

"Oh, yeah." Nate took a long drink, trying to will his racing heart to return to its rightful rhythm in his chest. "So I don't have anything to worry about as far as my niece is concerned?"

"You don't. If you did, then I'd tell you out of professional courtesy if nothing else."

"Thank you."

Adeline shifted in her seat. "This is my fault. I'm putting you all in danger. I should leave. Perhaps Mark can deliver on his promise and find me a room on his army base or something."

"You're not going anywhere." Nate spoke sharply and emphatically. He knew there was no point as she couldn't hear him, but did it anyway. It relived the tension filling him. "I have fought tooth and nail to get permission for you to stay here. And you're not going anywhere until we catch the killer."

"Just until forensics have finished with my house."

"Until the Herbalist is locked up," Nate repeated, signing at the same time. "I don't want anything to happen to you."

"Thank you."

"And once your house is handed back to you, I'll help you redecorate the hall, and change the carpet if that's what you want."

"Thank you. That would be good."

****

Over the course of the next week, Adeline settled into a routine. Nate went to work leaving her, Vianne, and Agent Debone in the house. She would go into work, taking Vianne and Shadow as Vianne insisted on calling the agent, with her. Vianne sat either at the desk coloring or by the dolls' beds reading to them, while Agent Debone followed Adeline's every move. It was tiresome, but she could see the reasoning behind it.

One thing she did enjoy was spending every

evening with Nate. Going to bed, knowing he was sleeping just down the hallway made her sleep better than she had since this whole nightmare began. But the best part happened on her first morning. She'd gotten up early to read her Bible in the kitchen over coffee as was her habit. Nate found her and asked if he could join her. They had spent an hour in reading and prayer every day since.

On Sunday Nate drove them all to church. Agent Debone hesitated at the door. "I might just keep watch from out here. There's only the one door, right?"

"There are fire exits at the back, and the three doors you can see here, but I thought you were supposed to keep me in your line of sight at all times."

"Miss Monroe, this would be the best way to proceed. Sgt. Holmes can go in with you, and I'll watch the road. I can call him if something happens."

"My phone is on silent," Nate told him. "But I'll change it to vibrate." He led Adeline inside. His hand was warm around hers, and the sensation of his skin against hers sent ripples of pleasure through her.

Mark stood on the door greeting people, and raised his eyebrow as he shook Nate's hand. "Morning, Sergeant. Is hand holding something you do with everyone you're protecting?"

Nate grinned. "Only your sister. I have a vested interest in protecting her. And it's Nate, please. We've known each other long enough to dispense with the formalities."

Mark hugged Adeline. "I wondered how long it'd be before you both figured it out, sis."

"Agent Debone isn't happy about it. Nate's boss won't be, either." She signed rather than spoke. "So please don't say anything to anyone just yet."

Mark mimed locking his lips and throwing away the key. "Agent Debone won't come in, then?"

Adeline shrugged. "We both tried. According to him, church is for fruitcakes."

"Really?" Mark grinned. "Maybe we should start serving that instead of biscuits with the tea and coffee after the service. Oh, and unless you want to start the gossip mill running full pelt, Nate, I'd let go of her hand before you go in. Too many little old ladies who love to spread the good news, if you get my drift."

Nate laughed and led Adeline and Vianne inside the building. "Was that a roundabout way of giving me his blessing to date you?"

"Yes. Mark is a man of few words unless he's displeased."

"Then I shall do my utmost not to displease him."

"That's probably a good move, considering what he does for a living."

Nate nodded in agreement. "He could probably teach my self-defense class better than I can. And out-shoot me."

****

Tuesday afternoon, Adeline looked up as the light flashed and the door opened.

A tall man stood there, long dreadlocks pulled back into a ponytail and a bandana tied over his head. Baggy trousers, waistcoat, and floppy sleeved shirt all in bright, clashing colors, meant it could only be one person. Susie's boyfriend, Storm.

Ben brushed past her as he backed away. Adeline glanced down, wondering what the problem was. He was a people dog and had never reacted like that before.

Not having time to worry over that, Adeline turned her attention to the man. "Can I help you?"

"I've come to pick up Susie."

Agent Debone rose. "I'll get her." He moved to the interior door and opened it.

Adeline studied the man.

He paced the floor, sweat lining his brow. His smile, even when Susie came into the room, never reached his eyes. He held out a hand to her. "Let's go."

Susie angled herself so Adeline could see her. "Have you met Dr. A? She runs the place here."

Taking a deep breath, the man held out a hand. "Pleased to meet you. I'm Storm."

"Adeline." The instant his hand touched hers, Adeline's vision blurred. Dark black energy shot into her, chilling her to the core. Her legs wobbled, but she was unable to move, his gaze hypnotizing her. Sheer evil shone from the dark eyes, yet she couldn't look away.

"Pleasure to meet you." His voice penetrated her mind.

She could hear him in her head almost as if she weren't deaf. *God help me.* As she prayed, the darkness lifted enough for her to feel Vianne tugging at her sleeve.

"Are you all right?"

"I'm fine."

"I can call Uncle Nate if you're not feeling well."

Does Nate realize how astute this child is? "I'm all right." She let go of Storm's hand and glanced at Susie. "Have fun, and I'll see you bright and early on Monday morning."

Adeline headed to the ladies room on wobbly legs.

Her stomach roiled, and her head pounded. She shut the door and collapsed against it, and then closed her eyes tight. Why had she reacted like that? She'd never been overwhelmed when meeting someone. It was as if evil oozed from his every pore.

She washed her hands with water as hot as she could bear, desperate to rid herself of every trace of him. Glancing into the mirror she could still see his eyes, drilling into her. She should text Susie, warn her. But say what? Your boyfriend gives me the creeps? Maybe just a general warning to be extra vigilant.

She shivered, and headed back to her office. Pulling her cardigan off the back of the door, she slid into it, cold despite the heat of the day.

A red mist descended rapidly over her, and she staggered forwards into her desk. Her arm knocked the lamp sideways sending a dozen things crashing to the floor. She gasped for breath, as through the crimson veil, strong hands clamped tightly around her neck.

A masked face leaned over her. The glittering eyes bored into her, holding her gaze even as her vision dimmed. Her hands rose to her throat, trying to push him off. "Please…"

His lips moved. "You're safe now, my love. No one can harm you now. You're free."

Rasping breaths, harder to breathe, then everything faded in slow motion.

Ben licked her face, and she opened her eyes to find herself lying on the floor.

Vianne sat holding her hand, and Agent Debone had the phone clamped to one ear, his lips moving rapidly.

Adeline struggled to sit up. "What happened?"

"You blacked out," Agent Debone said. He put his hand over the mouthpiece of the phone. "Ben barked and almost broke the door down to get our attention. I assume it was another one?"

Adeline nodded. "He called her 'my love.' He knew her."

"Was there anything else? Carpet under her, or grass?"

Adeline closed her eyes for a moment, trying to think. "No, I saw it as if I were her."

"OK, then. What was above him?"

"I don't know. His face was right in mine. Balaclava, dark eyes, and thick lips. There was something blue." She worried her bottom lip, trying to think. "There was blue around him."

"OK." He turned back to the phone.

Vianne touched her arm, and Adeline turned. "Are you all right, Adeline? Uncle Nate prays with me when I have a bad dream. It helps. Would you like me to do that for you?"

Tears filled Adeline's eyes. A huge lump choked her, and she nodded, beyond words.

Vianne grasped both her hands. "Dear, Lord Jesus. Please look after Adeline. She's very scared right now because of the nasty dream she just had. Put Your arms around her, hug her, and remind her just how much You love her. Thank you. Amen."

Adeline smiled at the simplicity of the prayer. "Thank you. That was lovely."

"It's the one Uncle Nate uses for me. It always works. Then he does this." She hugged Adeline tightly.

Adeline hugged her back.

After a moment, Vianne pulled back. "I redid my list of people for Uncle Nate to marry. You're top of it now."

"Oh, am I?"

Vianne nodded. "Sure are. He likes you a lot. He prays for you all the time."

"And you know this how?"

She shrugged. "I hear him when he doesn't think I'm still awake. He tells Jesus he loves you very much and is waiting for the right time to tell you. Do you like him too? Uncle Nate, that is. I already know you love Jesus."

"Yes, I do like Uncle Nate. Very much."

"Cool." Vianne smiled. "So, are you all right now?"

"I'm better."

Agent Debone touched her arm. "I need to get the both of you home, now."

"I'll lock up. But first I want to ring Susie."

"She's gone out with the creepy boyfriend," Vianne told her.

"I forgot to tell her something. I'll call and tell her." She stood and shakily reached for the phone. She dialed Susie's mobile, but it went straight to voice mail. "Susie, call me when you get this. It's important."

She put the phone down and grabbed Ben's lead. "Come on, then. Let's go home."

****

Adeline didn't feel like cooking, so she ordered pizza to be delivered.

Vianne went to bed at eight under protest, but with the condition Uncle Nate went up as soon as he got in.

Adeline was about to go to bed when the front door opened at ten. She looked at the tired man standing in the doorway. "Nate?"

He shut the door and turned to her. "Come and sit down."

"I don't want to sit."

Grief and something else radiated from him. "I think you should." He took her arm and gently led her into the lounge. He sat beside her, not releasing her hand. "The officers on watch in Olive Grove caught someone dumping a body just after six. Three hours after Agent Debone rang. I'm really sorry, Adeline. It was Susie."

Adeline doubled over as if she'd been punched in the gut. Tears poured down her face. "No...." Please, not Susie, too. Be with her family. She may have infuriated me at times, but she didn't deserve this. None of them did.

Nate gently raised her face. "It wasn't her boyfriend. It was a much older bloke. He must have had his hair cut recently as it was incredibly short. But he matched the CCTV pictures, and the ones you took of the Prime Minister's visit."

"So it's him...the Herbalist?"

"Yes."

"Are you sure?"

"Yes, Adeline, it's over. We've got him." His arms wrapped around her, and his cologne flooded her senses. Safe, she clung to him, tears of grief mixing with tears of relief.

12

Over the next ten days, life slowly reverted to normal. There were no more nightmares or visions.

The doll hospital closed for a few days to hold services both for Jasmine and Susie. Adeline returned to work after the funerals, still taking Vianne every day, as school holidays hadn't finished.

Mrs. Avon, the new receptionist, was a sweet old lady in her sixties. Past normal retirement age, the neat, white-haired lady needed something to fill her days after her husband died. A real blessing and grandmother figure, she was great with the kids. Adeline thanked God several times a day for bringing Mrs. Avon in at just the right time.

With Nate's help, Adeline repainted and re-carpeted the hall, landing, and stairs in her home. A pale lilac paint complimented the cream carpet. The whole house smelled of paint, but she moved home regardless. As much as she loved being at Nate's and spending each evening alone with him, she needed time in her own space to evaluate the way things had changed between them.

As each day passed, holding hands and exchanging burning kisses outside her bedroom door, made it harder and harder to say goodnight. The temptation to go further than they should wasn't fair on either of them. Moving back to her home gave them the space they needed.

"Have you got everything?" Nate let go of the bag handles and closed the trunk of the car.

"I have." Adeline let Ben jump on the back seat next to Vianne and shut the door, before getting in the front. "Are you really paintballing at work tomorrow?"

Nate fastened his seat belt and started the engine. He checked over his shoulder and pulled away from the curb. "Yup. They call it team bonding—but in this case, I think it's more to unwind and let off steam. The last bonding exercise we had to go on was an overnighter. We went out to the Chilterns and set up camp. There were four in my group, and none of us had put a tent up for years and these weren't even tents, more like tarps to cover us. Eventually we managed and after we'd eaten, we settled down to sleep. Some hours later, Peter Jones, the Chief Inspector woke up and then roused everyone else. He looked over at Dane, and said, "Sarge, look up at the sky and tell me what you see.""

Nate put the car into first gear as he approached the traffic lights. "Dane replied, "I see millions of stars, sir." The DCI looked askance at him, and demanded, "What does that tell you?" Well, Dane's a bit of a know-it-all, so he takes this as a chance to show up the rest of us. He took a deep breath and replied, "Astronomically speaking, it tells me that there are millions of galaxies, and potentially billions of planets. Astrologically, it tells me that Saturn is in Leo. Time wise, it appears to be approximately a quarter past three. Theologically, it is evident the Lord is all-powerful, and we are small and insignificant. Meteorologically, it seems we will have a beautiful day tomorrow. What does it tell you, sir?""

"He didn't..."

"Oh, he did. There was total silence for a moment, then the DCI gave him the most withering look you've ever seen. He cleared his throat and replied as dryly as he could, "Actually, Sergeant, it means that someone has stolen our tent.""

Adeline laughed. "You made that up."

Nate shook his head. "No, it really happened. Tell you, Dane's never, ever lived it down."

"I bet he didn't. So was it really stolen?"

"No. Six of the other blokes played a practical joke and took it down as we slept." Nate parked the car, and then went around to open the door for her. "Here we are. I'll carry your bags."

"I can manage."

"Just let me do the macho thing for once."

Adeline winked at him. "I'm sure you'll love that." She ran her gaze over his biceps. "Does this mean you're going to flex your muscles as well?"

Nate laughed and immediately struck a strong man pose.

Adeline felt his muscles. "He needs to practice," she said glancing back at Vianne. "Will you make sure he does?"

"Yes…" Vianne doubled over with laughter.

Nate pouted, and then planted a light kiss on Adeline's lips while Vianne wasn't looking.

She kissed him back. "I'm teasing."

"I know. And she'll make sure I practice now, you do realize that?"

"Good. You need it." She let Ben out of the car. She smiled at Vianne. "Are you still coming in to work with me tomorrow?"

"Sure I am. This is the best summer holidays ever."

Adeline gave her a thumbs-up. "See you tomorrow."

She followed Nate up the path and unlocked the door.

Ben ran in ahead, his tail wagging. "He's checking to make sure that everything's as he left it."

"He seems pleased to be home, too." Nate gripped her hand tightly. "Will you be all right?"

"We'll be fine."

He hugged her. "Then I'll see you in the morning when I drop Vianne off. Mrs. Avon offered to babysit sometime so we can go out on our own."

"Mrs. Avon wants to come on our dates?"

"I mean Vianne."

"I know that. That would be good. But sometimes we should take her as well."

"Vianne or Mrs. Avon?" Nate kissed her goodbye.

"Both," she laughed. She waved as he headed to the car.

Ben appeared demanding food.

She picked up her bags and shut the door.

****

Three days later, Adeline walked across the park, holding Nate's hand. He'd been quiet all evening, and she guessed he had something on his mind. They reached the brow of the hill and moved over to the bench. The rosy hue of the setting sun lit the sky as they sat down.

Vianne ran across the grass in front of them, throwing a stick to Ben.

Adeline put her hands on her lap and looked out over the park. "It's beautiful."

Nate's eyes sparkled in the orange light. "I can't believe you've never sat and watched the sunset here before."

"No. I never had the chance, and besides the park's not safe after dark."

He squeezed her hand, and tucked a stray strand of hair behind her ear. His fingers lingered on her cheek, his intent gaze triggering a response she wasn't prepared for. "This time it is."

"Of course. I have a police officer to protect me."

"Actually, I was thinking more along the lines of Ben looking after you and you protecting me. You can ward off any potential threats by hitting them with your handbag. Or you simply head-butt them."

"And have you arrest me for assault?"

He clicked his fingers. "Darn. I guess I'd have to. In that case, don't hit them. We'll just run away instead."

The sky flamed red and orange as the sunset deepened, reflecting in his eyes.

She rubbed her arms, and he touched her face to get her attention. "Are you cold? We can walk a bit more if you'd like. Head back to the car slowly."

"Sure."

Nate pulled her upright and slid his hand into hers. "Vianne, we're walking. Come on."

She obediently ran over to him. "Where are we going?"

"We're heading back to the car."

"But I wanted to play on the swings. You said it was safe, 'cos the bad man is locked up."

"I did, but it's getting late now."

She pouted. "Fine."

"You can go on ahead with Ben, just put him back

on the leash. And stay where I can see you."

Vianne did as she was told and walked off, muttering.

Nate shook his head. "Kids."

"She'll get over it. You've got warm hands, unlike mine."

"You know what they say, cold hands, warm heart. Does that make me cold-hearted?"

She shook her head. "I don't think so. You couldn't be cold-hearted if you tried."

The last vestiges of the sunset faded as he led her back across the park to the car. "Is that a dare?"

"It can be if you want."

"No, it's fine. It was Pete who took dares, I was the sensible one, apparently. But, I could get used to this."

"Used to what?"

He unlocked the car. "Being with you. We missed you. I missed you. The house isn't the same without you in it."

"I've missed you, too. But you know why I had to go. It's not right that we live together, even if we have separate rooms. I'm not just thinking of your reputation, either. The temptation is just too much."

"I know."

"Besides, I like this dating thing. It's nice."

Nate grinned and opened the door for her. "It is. If I can get a sitter for tomorrow night, would you like dinner? I found somewhere that accepts service dogs."

"I'd like that."

"Cool—dress smart."

They drove for a while before Vianne poked her.

Adeline pulled down the sun visor to read the child's lips.

"My watch pinged. It's bath time."

"Your watch did what?" It looked like 'ponged', but that made no sense.

Vianne showed her. "It pings when it's bath time."

"Then we should get you home. We have to work in the morning."

Vianne bounced up and down in the car seat. "Yay. It's Wednesday and pay day."

"Pay day?" Nate looked askance at Adeline. "You pay her?"

"Sure I do. Would you prefer I used child exploitation and didn't pay her?"

"Not really. So how much an hour do you get paid, pumpkin?"

Vianne's eyes lit up. "You get paid hourly?"

"Grown-ups do. You get paid weekly in comics and coloring books." Adeline said, then laughed.

"And colors. I get that pen set tomorrow with sixty-four colors in it."

"Really?" Nate raised an eyebrow. "If that's the one you've been hounding me for weeks, it's not cheap."

"You know how much a real assistant would cost me, Nate? Vianne's having fun, she's kept busy, and I'm quid's in. It's not hurting anyone. Besides, she's learning she has to earn stuff." The car stopped outside her house. "Thank you very much. I'll see you both in the morning."

"I'll walk you to the door. Stay here, kiddo."

"There's no need." She kissed his cheek. "Goodnight."

****

Adeline spent the whole day anticipating dinner.

She had a light breakfast and skipped lunch. Ten minutes before closing, Ben alerted her to the ringing phone. "Datura Doll Hospital."

"Hey, it's Nate. I'm really sorry, but I'm going to have to cancel. Something's come up at work, and I'm going to be here a while yet."

She hid the stab of regret. "No problem. Do you want me to take Vianne home with me?"

"Yes, please. Actually, could you take her to my place? I have no idea what time I'm going to finish tonight, so I cancelled the baby-sitter. Feel free to crash on the sofa or in the spare room if I'm not home by eleven."

"OK."

"I'm really, really sorry."

"Me, too." She hung up and looked at the phone. She closed her eyes, attempting to tamp down the disappointment. *Let's take this and turn it into a positive.*

Ben tapped her leg, and Adeline opened her eyes to see Vianne standing the other side of the desk. "Hey."

"Are you all right?"

"I'm fine. That was Uncle Nate on the phone. He's been held up at work so he's going to be really late tonight."

The child's face fell. "Again? But you were going out to dinner."

"I know and I'm disappointed, but I was thinking. Why don't instead of going out, you and I go home via the precinct and get some fish and chips and eat them out of the paper at your house. We could make a den under the dining table if you like."

"Can we have salt and vinegar on the chips?"

"Is there any other way to have them?" Adeline

reached for her bag. "Come on, let's go."

****

Trying to get Vianne out from the den at bedtime was a losing battle.

Adeline soon gave up and fetched duvet and pillows and let her fall asleep under the table. Just after eleven, she locked the front door and snuggled down on the couch under a blanket. She left the side table lamp on in case Vianne woke.

She opened her eyes, heart racing, as Ben jumped on her and licked her face.

"What's up?"

He leapt down and ran to the door, pausing to look back at her.

"OK, I'm coming."

Adeline rubbed her eyes and looked at the clock. Two AM. She must have fallen asleep, but who would it be at this time of night? And why hadn't Nate gotten up?

Holding her breath, she peered through the spy hole. Nate. That would be why he hadn't answered the door.

He slid inside as she opened the door. "Thanks. I thought I'd have to sleep in the car for a moment."

"Did you lose your key?"

"No. You must have put the deadbolt across."

"Oh, I'm sorry. It's force of habit. Good thing Ben heard you."

Nate nodded and petted Ben. "It was. No harm done. How's Vianne?"

"She's fast asleep in her den under the table. I saved you some dinner, but you look exhausted."

"I am. I'm just going to go to bed." He hugged and kissed her gently. "Goodnight."

"Goodnight."

Nate locked the front door and peeped into the lounge at Vianne, before heading up the stairs. He looked dead on his feet, and Adeline wouldn't have been surprised if he'd curled up on the stairs and slept there.

She headed back into the lounge and lay under the blanket. She closed her eyes, a sudden burden of prayer for Nate coming over her.

When she finally did fall asleep, she dreamed she was running from something she couldn't see. A storm surrounded her, and she was alone. Above her shone dark, slitted eyes, following her every move, and a stench of garlic oozed from the ground she stood on. She woke, drenched in sweat, gasping for breath. Why were the dreams back? He was locked up now, she and every other woman was safe. Weren't they?

****

The following day, Nate called to say he'd be late again.

Adeline closed the shop and took Vianne home. He'd looked drained that morning before he left for work. She'd wanted to discuss the dream with him, but the moment had come and gone so fast, she hadn't.

Ben alerted her to the door, just as she put the shepherd's pie in the oven. Opening it, she found a well-dressed woman, with two bags by her feet. Wondering what she was selling, Adeline plastered a smile on her face. "Can I help you?"

The woman's face turned to stone as her gaze ran

over Adeline's apron and disheveled appearance. "Who are you? Where's Nathaniel?"

Nathaniel? Did she mean Nate? "Nate isn't back from work yet."

Vianne pushed past her and hugged the lady.

"I'm fine, Vianne, sweetheart," she replied, only confusing Adeline further. "How are you?"

Adeline couldn't see the response until Vianne turned around. "This is Adeline. I work with her sometimes, and she's Uncle Nate's friend. This is my Nanny. Grandad's just coming with the bags. Adeline can't hear you unless you look at her. She's deaf."

"I see. Are you Nathaniel's girlfriend?"

Adeline paused, not having put their relationship into those terms. Before she could answer, Nate's mother pushed past her and into the house.

"Yes, dear." The tall man, who followed her into the hall with another bag, bore a striking resemblance to Nate. He nodded to his wife and held out a hand to Adeline. "Jeremiah Holmes. It's a pleasure to meet you—?"

"Adeline Monroe." She shook his hand. His touch was cold, almost clinical.

"Have you known Nate long?"

"A while. We go to the same church." She shut the door and looked at the bags. "He didn't tell me you were coming."

"He doesn't know. Libby decided this morning, and he wasn't answering his phone when we rang."

"He's really busy at work right now, but he does pick up his messages on his mobile."

"His mobile?" Libby's face filled with disgust. "We don't use those. Landlines are quite sufficient."

"Do you want me to make up the spare room for

you?"

"I'll do it." Libby paused at the foot of the stairs and gave her a withering glance. "I trust I'm not pushing you out of your bed? I assume you *are* sleeping in the spare bed if you're staying here?"

"I don't live here. I have my own place." Adeline's face burned. Bile rose at the insinuation, and she swallowed hard. "I'm just looking after Vianne until Nate gets home."

"Good." She stuck out a hand. "Lady Elizabeth Holmes, I assume my husband already introduced himself, but he's Lord Holmes."

Shock followed hard on the heels of discomfort and humiliation. *Lady Holmes? Why hadn't Nate said he and his parents were titled? Do I have to curtsey?*

She recovered quickly, not wanting to lose face any more than she already had. "Adeline Monroe. It's nice to meet you."

Vianne looked at Adeline and signed. "Uncle Nate is a Sir, but he hates it, and won't use it. I guess I was a lady before Daddy died, but I'm glad I'm not. Ladies have to behave."

Lady Holmes reached out and grasped Vianne's hands. "Stop doing that, Vianne. It's as rude as whispering. Well, Miss Monroe, we're here now and won't take up any more of your valuable time. I'm sure you have other things you'd much rather be doing. Say goodbye, Vianne."

Vianne pulled free of her grandmother and hugged Adeline. "Bye, Adeline." Dropping back into sign language she said, "I don't want you to go."

Adeline signed back, speaking aloud for the benefit of Nate's parents. "It's OK. I'll see you tomorrow. You're getting really good at signing."

"I have a good teacher." Vianne frowned as she stumbled over the signs.

"Well done. Say hi to Uncle Nate when he gets in." Adeline signed slowly as she spoke so Vianne could follow.

"I will." Vianne hugged her.

Adeline hugged her back. She clipped on Ben's leash and straightened. "It's nice to have met you both. There's a shepherd's pie in the oven and veggies cooking on the stove. It should be ready in about fifteen minutes."

"Thank you. Goodbye."

The door shut in her face, and Adeline stood there in a daze for a few seconds. Had she just been thrown out? It certainly seemed that way. How did someone as nice as Nate, have such an awful mother?

She looked down at Ben. "Come on. Let's go home."

Starting to walk, her mind in turmoil, she realized she'd left her phone on the kitchen counter.

"Never mind. Perhaps Nate will see it and bring it to the doll hospital tomorrow when he drops Vianne off," She told Ben. "If not, I'll have to get it later."

Nothing would come of the fledgling relationship with Nate. Titled lords didn't date or marry the hoi polloi.

Especially not a deaf commoner like her. It wasn't until she got home, she realized she no longer thought of herself as plump. At least one good thing had come from the short lived relationship with Nate.

13

Just after dusk, Nate pulled onto the drive, his heart sinking as he recognized his parents' car. He checked his phone. No, he hadn't missed a message saying they were coming. He loved them dearly, just wished they'd warn him before arriving on his doorstep. He could at least tidy the house that way. Not to mention steel himself for his mother's inevitable comments on his parenting skills, or lack thereof.

She hadn't been happy with Pete's decision to make him Vianne's legal guardian. But Pete had done it for a reason. And honestly, Nate didn't blame him at all. Their childhood hadn't been easy at the best of times. Pete got the worst of it as he was the eldest son. But since Pete's death, he was the sole heir of his father's title and the country estate, and the sole focus of his mother's scorn. She had a set idea about how a Lord, or Lord-in-waiting, should behave. And a cop wasn't it.

The front door opened as he reached it. The smell of roast venison wafted over him.

"Nanny and Grandad are here," Vianne said. "They came to stay."

"So I see."

"She's in the kitchen, redoing dinner. Adeline and I made you shepherd's pie, but that's..." she broke off and checked over her shoulder before finishing in a whisper, "...peasant food."

He stifled his reaction. "Come here and give me a hug."

"Adeline went home." Vianne said as she stepped into his embrace. "Nanny didn't want her here. She asked if she were pushing Adeline out of her bed, when she offered to make up the spare room, assuming she slept in there. But Adeline isn't staying here at the moment and even when she did she had her own room, just like I do."

Nate froze, his already taut body tightening even further. His mother had implied *what?* "I'm sorry?"

"Did I say something wrong?"

"No, sweetheart. You didn't say anything wrong."

"OK."

"And you're right. Adeline did have her own room. Just like you do." And for that he was grateful. He looked concerned as his niece rubbed her stomach. "Are you OK?"

"I like shepherd's pie," she whispered. "Don't like what Nanny's making. And I'm hungry. My tummy hurts."

"Haven't you eaten yet?" He looked at his watch. It was almost seven forty-five.

"No."

"I'll sort it. Go watch TV while I talk to her."

"OK." She ran off.

Nate took a deep breath and pushed to his feet. He hung his coat on the rack and headed into the kitchen. "Hi."

His mother turned. "Nathaniel, you're late."

He bristled, feeling the hair stand on end on the back of his neck. "I had a lot of work on today." He kissed her cheek. "I didn't realize you were coming."

"Apparently, it's a good thing we did. Vianne's

picked up all sorts of bad habits from that dreadful babysitter of yours. Including some strange hand waving and eating habits. Of all the people to leave my grandchild with you could have picked someone better. This woman can't even hear her if something happens."

"Adeline is not my babysitter. She's a very good friend," he said stiffly. "And as for her being deaf and using sign language, Vianne's not the only one who uses it." He looked at her, continuing in sign. "I do as well."

"And like I told Vianne, that's as rude as whispering."

Nate turned to his father. "Hi, Dad."

Dad shook his hand. "Nate. Sorry to drop in unannounced, but once your mother gets an idea in her head, it's best to go with it."

"How was the drive?"

"It would have been a lot easier without your mother constantly complaining that we hadn't let Jeeves drive us."

"You know how much I dislike you driving," Mum interrupted. "What's the point of having a chauffeur if you don't use him? The same goes for a cook. Perhaps we could send for Mrs. Jones. Have her cook for us while we're here. Jeeves could bring her."

"And they would sleep where?" Nate asked. "Did you want them to share a room? Or are you planning on kicking Vianne out of her room again?"

"It's only right she make way for guests."

"And speaking of guests, I asked Adeline to look after Vianne until I got back from work. Vianne said you sent her home." He glanced around. "And that Adeline already made dinner."

"That's in the fridge cooling. Then it can go in the freezer. I'm doing you a proper dinner."

"Please don't throw my guests out again," Nate said evenly. "Vianne doesn't like venison."

"She'll eat what she's given."

Nate strode to the fridge and pulled out the dish of shepherd's pie. He yanked open the drawer and grabbed a spoon. "She can have what Adeline made."

"You spoil that child." Mum's tone was filled with venom. "She'd be better off with us."

"Why's that? So a nanny can look after her and a governess can teach her?"

"We'd find her a nice boarding school."

Nate's temper was rising despite his best intentions. He'd not even been in the same room with her ten minutes, and already his mother had riled him to almost the point of no return. "She's ten years old."

"You went to boarding school when you were five."

"Don't I know it," Nate snapped. He shoved the plate into the microwave.

"You're not really going to feed her that? It's peasant food."

"She likes it. It's simply beef and potatoes cooked a different way." He started reheating the food. "And no disrespect intended, Mum, but this is *my* house. Vianne is in *my* care and I'll bring her up how I like."

He could almost see the hackles rise as Mum drew herself up into what Pete had irreverently, but lovingly, referred to as 'grumbly mummy'. "Oh, really?"

"Yes, really."

"And does that include exposing her to a long string of unsuitable girlfriends? She said Adeline had been sleeping here."

"Yes, Adeline stayed here while her place was being redecorated."

"Didn't she have family she could stay with?"

"Not that I owe you an explanation, but someone was murdered in her home and the department decided she needed to be protected and not be with her family, in case there was another attempt on her life. Another police officer stayed here, not just when I was working, but overnight as well. We were already friends, so it seemed the best solution to everyone."

"I thought you were different than Peter. He always fell for the wrong kind of girl. Did you know he only married that French woman because she was pregnant?"

"*What?*"

"Of course we insisted, I mean you can't have the earl's son born out of wedlock. When she left him, we weren't surprised. We hoped he'd file for divorce and find someone more suitable. Of course, it didn't happen, so now we have to pin our hopes on you. You need to make the right choice in a woman. Someone classy, with bearing, and their own money. Definitely not someone who'll marry you for your title and because you're rich."

"So that rules Adeline out, I suppose?"

"Well she's hardly pretty is she? She might be if she lost a few pounds, but her deafness really put's paid to her usefulness." Mum lowered her voice. "I mean, what would her children turn out like?"

Nate's hands clenched into fists. "She wasn't born deaf. She caught measles when she was five. Her hearing loss was a complication from being sick. And I'll decide my choice of bride when the time comes."

Lord, God, help me here. I don't want things to get any more uncomfortable than they are. I'm not going to tell her no one knows about the title... He broke off. *Well I guess Adeline does now.* He pulled the plate from the microwave and took it to the table. "Vianne, dinner," he called.

Her answering call was accompanied by running footsteps.

"Wash your hands," Mum told her.

Vianne turned on the taps, spraying water all over the draining board. "Can I have ketchup with it? Can you make it a cross face this time?"

Ignoring the hiss of disgust from his mother, Nate nodded. "Sure. So long as you eat all of it. Including the green stuff."

Vianne dried her hands. "I already promised Adeline that."

He kissed her forehead and drew ketchup in the shape of a cross face on her dinner. "Good girl. Now say grace and you can eat."

"Time was a child had to wait until everyone was ready to eat," his mother said.

"She has a set routine. Tea at six, seven at the latest, and bed at eight-thirty. It suits both of us."

"I thought I raised you better than this." His mother's voice quivered and he knew it was part of her act to try to make him feel guilty.

"You didn't raise me at all," he snapped. "Five nannies did."

His father's hand descended on his shoulder. "That's enough."

Nate sent a silent prayer to God asking for patience. His mother tried it at the best of times. "Sorry, Mum."

She huffed. "Dinner will be ten minutes. I suggest

you go shower and change."

Vianne shot him a slight smile and angling her hands so her grandmother couldn't see them, signed to him. "Guess you're ten, too."

He signed back, not caring if his mother noticed. "Always a child in here." He pointed to his heart. "Be right back," he finished aloud.

Ten minutes later, he came back into the kitchen, reluctantly admitting his mother's suggestion of a shower made him feel more human. He sat down and said grace. He picked up his knife and fork. He had to concede the meal smelt and looked inviting. But given a choice, he'd rather have what Adeline had made for him.

"Adeline left her phone here," Vianne told him. "It's on top of the biscuit jar."

"I'll take it over after you're in bed," he said. "Nanny and Grandad can look after you for a few minutes."

His mother shook her head. "There was something we wished to discuss with you tonight."

"Adeline needs her phone."

"Oh, Nathaniel, really. The woman is deaf. How can a deaf person need or even use a telephone?"

"A new invention called text messaging. It's like email." He cut into his meat. "Therefore, she needs this one."

"Fine. But we need to have a discussion before you go."

Nate shoved down his annoyance. "OK."

14

Furious with his mother, Nate drove to Adeline's place in a rage.

He knew he was the heir to the title. He also knew his mother's feelings on the subject of his job. Apparently his actions over the past few weeks had given them cause for concern. It didn't help being headline news over the shooting of the Prime Minister or in the Herbalist case.

The end result was his parents demanded he quit the police force. They didn't bother to ask or suggest, but rather ordered him to resign. Give up the job he loved, move back to the country estate and learn how the business was run, so that he would be ready to take over when something happened to his father.

He clenched his hands around the steering wheel. He had no intentions of quitting. He'd pointed out that diving on top of a woman being shot at was part of his job. If he wanted to sit behind a desk, he'd work in a call center. That just made things escalate into a shouting match he was amazed hadn't woken Vianne. In which the subject of marriage and children had once more been raised.

Finally tired of the harassment, Nate took action.

Needing to get out before he lost his temper completely, he'd snatched up Adeline's phone. "I'll be back late, so don't wait up." He slammed the door as he went out.

As he parked the car, guilt flooded him. He buried his head in his hands and prayed for forgiveness. His mother had no right to treat Adeline the way she had, or to lecture him as if he were a small child, but he had no right to speak to her the way he did. By doing so, he'd broken one of the commandments, if not more than one.

He walked up the path and rang the bell. The house was in semi-darkness, and he half expected Adeline to have gone to bed.

Adeline's face fell as she opened the door. Ben wagged his tail by her side.

"Hi, Adeline."

"Hi. I didn't think I'd see you tonight...Sir Holmes."

Nate closed his eyes for a moment, a sharp sword piercing his heart. "I know I should have told you. I'm sorry."

"It's fine." Her tone along with her stiff signing proved to him it was anything but fine.

He needed to put things right between them before he went home and dealt with his mother. "It's not fine. Can I come in and talk for a moment?"

She shook her head, starting to close the door.

He shoved his foot in and folded his hand over the edge of the door. "Please, Adeline. Just five minutes. I brought your phone back." He held it out like a carrot.

"Five minutes." Adeline opened the door. She took the phone. "Thank you."

"You're welcome." He took a deep breath. "I owe you an apology."

"Why? Did you phone the Australian speaking clock on my phone for a couple of hours before you gave it back to me?"

He chuckled despite the torment flooding him. "No. But leave your phone in my house again, and I might just do that."

"You can afford the phone bill."

He raised a hand and rubbed the back of his neck. "I should have told you, but I was afraid your opinion of me would change."

"I'm sorry?"

"I thought, however misguided it may have been, that if you found out I was not only rich, but came with a title and a country estate, you'd throw yourself at me. Once I got to know you, I knew it wouldn't, but by that point I didn't know how to tell you."

"Why would I only want to know you because of your money?"

"Because it happened with Pete. Once girls knew who he was they flocked to his side. Ophelié included." He rubbed the back of his neck. "Mum told me tonight that Pete only married her because she was pregnant."

Adeline's cool hand touched his overheated one. "I'm sorry."

"I never thought Pete would be that irresponsible, but I guess you never really know a person."

"I know you. And you're a proper gentleman."

"Thank you."

Her fingers traced the outline of his jaw. "However, I don't think your mother likes me or wants you mixing with commoners."

Nate kissed her. "My mother doesn't approve of me and my job, full stop. But I'm a big boy now and can choose my own friends. I happen to like you and like spending time with you."

"The feeling's mutual." She kissed him back.

"I know it's late, but do you want to go for a walk?"

Late August meant the nights were drawing in and getting chilly.

"In the dark and the cold?" She rubbed her hands over her arms, pretending to shiver. "It's a full moon, there'll be werewolves out tonight."

"You'll have your own personal police escort."

"Oh in that case, as you put it so nicely, sure we'll come for a walk." She put Ben's leash on him and slid into her jacket. Picking up her keys, she shut and locked the front door behind her.

Nate took her free hand in his as they started walking down the road.

"How was your day?"

"Not too bad, all things considered. After work Vianne and I did some shopping and we cooked dinner at your place. Then your parents arrived. So, I went home and cleaned the house. How was your day?"

"Frustrating. I spent the morning in court only to have the judge throw the case out because of some screw-up by the CPS."

"The what?"

Nate turned his head so she could see him pronounce the words he wasn't sure how to sign. "CPS. Crown Prosecution Service."

"Ah. It isn't the Herbalist case they threw out, is it?"

"No. Then I get back to my desk to find half the files I need for next week's court case are missing, and then I ended up being called into the field. I finally got home to discover my parents have come to stay for a week and thrown my girlfriend out of my house."

Adeline raised an eyebrow. "You have a girlfriend? You never told me."

"Didn't I? That was very remiss of me. Yes Adeline, I have a girlfriend."

"We should introduce her to my boyfriend."

He laughed. "Now there's a thought. We could double date."

"Maybe we should. It would give your mother something to talk about."

"I can see her face now, actually. You know, I love her to bits, I just wish she'd back off sometimes and not interfere."

"It's part of a mother's job description. Mark says it's found in the caring section, paragraph seven, subsection five. Thou shalt interfere at least six times a day, as thy child knows nothing and wilt not listen anyway." She squeezed his hand. "Thing is we listen, and choose not to accept their advice sometimes. They might not like it, but it's what we have to do."

He squeezed her hand back. "And she's not right about you."

"She loves you, Nate. She's just trying to look out for you."

"For the title more like."

Adeline stopped and turned towards him. "No, she loves *you* for who you are. That much was obvious. She just doesn't show it the way you'd like."

"She never has. Palmed us off on one nanny after another, questions how I'm raising Vianne…"

She lifted a finger and put it on his lips. "Shh. You are doing a wonderful job with Vianne. That little girl dotes on you. The day I first met her, she wouldn't tell me her name, despite how upset she was, because you'd told her never to give her name to strangers."

"Seriously? She told me that was a stupid rule."

"But she kept it none-the-less. Just because you don't agree with your parents' way of doing things, doesn't mean you don't respect their views. Or stop loving them. Just means as a grown up you have the option of disregarding them and going with your heart. Hence the two different commandments. 'Children obey your parents' in Ephesians, and the main one to 'honor your father and mother'."

"You know, you make a lot of sense." Nate pulled her close. "You just have a different way of looking at things. Another reason I love you." He kissed her nose.

The moon shone high in the sky, sending its silvery light down over the road as she kissed him back. Her fingers traced the outline of his jaw. "The full moon always reminds me of the poem about the highway man. You'd make a good one."

"I'd make a good highwayman?" he asked, not sure whether to be astonished or horrified.

Her fingers trailed through his hair. "Yeah, with your dark wavy hair and rugged handsome looks."

"You mean five o'clock shadow and bags under my eyes?"

"Yeah, them as well, but mainly your rugged, handsome looks." She gasped as he picked her up and stood her on a bench. She immediately tried to climb down, her cheeks glowing, one booted foot sliding off the edge of the bench. "What are you doing? Let me down."

"No, no stay there." His hand held her in place. "Untie your hair."

"I reckon the stress of work has finally gone to your head, but OK." Adeline pulled the band from her hair, letting it flow over her shoulders.

Nate backed away a few steps.

A quizzical expression crossed her face. "What are you doing?"

"I'm the highwayman, and you're Bess, the landlord's daughter."

"You're mad, but all right." She laughed as Nate first petted an invisible horse, then imitated climbing on to it, and galloped over to her.

Nate raised an imaginary whip and proceeded to rap on the shutters and as she pretended to open the window, he shot her the biggest grin he could manage. He recited the words of the poem, and then unable to reach to do the next part, he jumped up to stand on the bench beside her. He ran his fingers through her hair. It wasn't black, so he changed the next line of the poem. "Sweet blonde waves in the moonlight," he whispered, bending his face towards hers.

Adeline's dark eyes sparkled in the moonlight as he touched her hair. She leaned into his touch. "Nate…"

"He kissed its waves in the moonlight." He breathed in deep, taking in the scent of her shampoo and perfume, his hands running down her arms. "Adeline…" he whispered, kissing her hair, catching the top of her ear as well.

She shivered at his touch. "Is this where you gallop away to the west to be killed?"

"Not planning on it." He tilted her head and brushed his lips gently over hers.

She pulled back. "Nate, please. We're standing on a bench in the middle of a park."

He backed off instantly. "You're right, I'm sorry. I don't know what I was thinking." He got down and took her hand to help her down.

She jumped down off the bench, but didn't let go of his hand. "Don't be sorry. I didn't say I didn't want you to kiss me, just didn't want to be on display."

He glanced around them. "There's no one else here. We're alone in a park in the moonlight." His breath hung in the crisp still night air. He pulled her close again. "Now we're not standing on a bench, may I kiss you?" He moved closer, kissing her gently.

Not sure where she ended and he began, Nate felt the warmth of her body pressed against his, the gentle touch of her hands on his back and arms. He closed his eyes, setting aside conscious thought, and caught her bottom lip in his, deepening the kiss but keeping it gentle, showing her how much he loved her. His hands and arms wrapped themselves around her, pulling her as close to him as possible.

When they finally broke for air, Nate held on to her, his eyes not letting up from holding hers. His fingers gently caressed her face. "You OK?"

She nodded. "More than OK. It was amazing. You gave me goose bumps." She tugged his hand and sat on the bench, pulling him down beside her. "Though my knees are decidedly weak and don't want to take my weight anymore."

Nate smiled, moving his fingers through her hair, not losing the eye contact. "You're beautiful," he said. He ran his thumb gently across her lips, noticing the way she shivered as he touched her. He brushed his lips against hers, his hands caressing her back and neck, aware of her taste, her scent, and the touch of her hands.

For a while nothing mattered as the two of them just sat lost in each other's arms and the feelings they had for each other. Finally Nate pulled back and looked at her. "I love you, Adeline. I have honestly never felt about anyone the way I feel about you."

Adeline laid a hand on top of his. "I love you, too. You make me feel complete, in a way I never thought possible."

Nate was convinced she was the woman God intended him to spend the rest of his life with. It felt right in his heart, in that place where he spoke with God and prayed. He slid off the bench. Getting down on one knee, he took her hand and gazed up at her.

"Adeline, I love you, all of you. Would you do me the honor of marrying me?"

Her eyes widened. "Marry?"

"Yes, marry." He let go of her hand and signed as he spoke. "Marry me, be my wife. You are my soul mate."

Her face broke into a huge smile, and she signed a reply. "Yes, I'd love to marry you. But what about your mother? And the fact you're titled and I'm not."

"I don't want you to marry my mother." He sat and wrapped his arms around her. "I want you to marry me. And as for the title? I inherit it eventually. It won't change who I am or where I live or what I do. Or who I love."

****

Still walking on air, Adeline strolled up the path to her front door, Nate's hand securely in hers. He loved her, all of her. She'd meet his parents properly tomorrow and then they could start planning the rest of their lives together. She unlocked her door. Before she had a chance to push it open, his arms were around her for a long, slow, tender kiss. Once more, her head spun and her whole body flamed. She hadn't dreamed such feelings could be evoked from a kiss.

She waved goodbye and closed the front door. She unfastened Ben's leash and hung it on the hook in the hallway. It slipped off and fell to the floor. She bent down and grabbed it. "No, you need to stay on the hook," she told it, looping it over again. "There, that's better. Now stay there."

Ben ran over to something on the floor and sniffed at it, before backing away.

"What have you got there?" Adeline picked up the padded envelope with her name and address on it. Turning it over, she looked for a post mark or return address.

Ripping it open she reached inside, pulling out a clear plastic bag.

Terror flooded her.

The bag contained dried herbs.

She dropped the bag and fumbled for the latch. Her hands shook. *Oh, God, please, don't let him be in the house. Please let Nate be out there.*

Nate was just getting into his car.

Running like the wind, Adeline left the house, screaming his name at the top of her lungs. "Nate!"

15

Over breakfast the following morning, Nate studied his fiancée across the table. His heart was full to bursting with so many different emotions. He fluctuated between ecstatic and worried and scared. As if, even now, some*thing* or some*one* might reach out and snatch away his happiness and chance of everlasting love.

Who had left the herbs? Was it a copycat? Was it just someone with a sick and ill-timed sense of humor? Or was there something more sinister going on?

But he had a sickening feeling they'd missed something. He had to get the Herbalist back in the interview room. The bag of herbs left at every murder had never been publicized. Nor would it be. But someone outside of the investigation team knew.

After Adeline had found the herbs, he'd brought her and Ben straight back to his house and sent a forensic team over to hers.

Preliminary results showed there had been no sign of forced entry and nothing had been touched. Even though it looked as if the envelope had just been shoved through the letter box, he wasn't going to take any chances. The herbs were at the lab, and the envelope being dusted for fingerprints. His fervent prayer was that there would be some trace of DNA or something that would give them a lead.

His mother hadn't been happy when he arrived

home with Adeline, the dog, and a suitcase. Given time he hoped she'd come around.

My fiancée. That has such a lovely ring to it, Lord. And speaking of rings, I need to do that at lunchtime today. I can't lose her now, I just can't. Keep her safe.

Adeline put her spoon down. "I know that look, Nate. Spit it out."

"Spitting is disgusting." Vianne interjected as she finished her toast.

"It is. Now go and wash your face. You have peanut butter all over it." Nate shot her a half smile.

"OK." She grinned at her grandparents. "You really should try peanut butter. Adeline thinks it's disgusting, but Uncle Nate and I like it."

Mum picked up her coffee cup. "Then I guess Miss Monroe and I agree on one thing"

Dad winked at Vianne. "You both get it from me. Just don't tell Nanny I like peanut butter, or she won't let me kiss her."

Mum shook her head. "Too late, I heard."

"In that case…" He reached for another slice of toast and the peanut butter.

Vianne laughed as she skipped from the room.

Nate stifled a grin and turned back to Adeline. "I've arranged backup and for a protection officer to follow you around today. However, I want to emphasize that I'm *not* happy with you going to work. At all—that's *Not* with a capital *N*. I'd far rather you stayed here, today and every day, until we catch him."

Steel flashed in her eyes, and a resolute look settled over her face. "I'm not giving in to him. I assume it was dried nettle in the bag," Adeline said, not signing.

"It was actually a combination of all the herbs with

datura added. He wants you dead." He signed to get his point across, speaking aloud so his parents understood, too.

"I thought you had the Herbalist locked up."

"Someone knows. Therefore the case is now active again and you're back in the protection system."

"Wonderful. Tell you one thing, if this guy, whoever he is, wants me dead, then he's going to have a fight on his hands," Adeline replied firmly. "We went over and over the self-defense stuff last night, until I can do it in my sleep. I have Ben and the officer following me around. We'll be fine."

"Hmmm." Somehow, despite the fact she'd broken his nose on her first attempt at the self-defense, that didn't make him feel any better. "Speaking of sleep. Did you dream last night?"

A tinge of something flickered in her eyes, then vanished. "I might have. I did the night before."

"And—?" Nate held her gaze, leaning across the table. He knew evasion when he saw it. He knew her concern, too. His parents would wonder what kind of person she was, with visions and dreams. But this was too important.

Mum set down her cup with an audible chink. "Nathaniel, really. I hardly think the breakfast table is the place for one of your interrogations."

"Mum, please. This is important. Adeline, did you dream about him?"

"Yes, all right. I did dream, but I don't know if it was him, or not. I dreamt I was running from something. There was a storm, lots of lightning and this huge pair of yellow eyes, like a cat's, with huge slits, watching me from the clouds. The ground stank of garlic. But, honestly, the garlic was the only real link."

"When was this?"

"Night before last was the first time. I would have told you yesterday morning at breakfast, but you looked shattered, and then your phone rang and you had to dash off." She rubbed the back of her neck. "I should have told you. I'm sorry."

Nate ran the pad of his thumb over her knuckles, his skin warming at the touch. "The first time?"

"I had it twice last night. It's probably nothing. It's not like before when I saw him killing. It's more of an overpowering sense of evil. Like something, or someone, is watching me all the time. And a storm. There is always a storm."

"Always tell me these things. I'm never too busy for you."

"OK. I'm sorry. I promise I will next time."

"Apology accepted." He smiled at her to show he wasn't mad at her. "PC Denise Jones will be joining Mrs. Avon on the front desk, this morning. Agent Debone is insisting on helping as well. He'll be in later. Two plain clothes officers will be outside in a parked car—"

"That's overkill. Seriously, Nate, that's far too much. By all means put someone on the inside, but other than that I don't need anyone there."

Nate sighed. She could be the most exasperating woman at times. "Adeline, be reasonable. I want to marry you, not bury you!"

Two pairs of eyes swung his way, two voices speaking at the same time.

"Marry?"

"You want to *what?*"

He glanced at his parents, having forgotten for a

moment they were both there. This wasn't how he wanted them to find out, but now it was done. "Yes, I intend to marry Adeline. I asked her last night, and she said yes. Although if I'd known then how pig-headed she is, I might have thought twice about it."

Adeline took his hand and squeezed it. "You know very well how stubborn I am, and you still love me. I promise, I'm going to marry you. I won't do anything to jeopardize it."

"Then let me post as many officers around you as I can. Especially in light of the dreams."

"See, I knew you'd react like this. That's why I hesitated over telling you about them."

His mother sent him a withering glance, making him feel ten years old again. "Adeline is a big girl, Nathaniel." She knew he preferred Nate. "If she wants to go to work, then let her. She'll be fine with all those officers around her. You worry far too much. Your father never mollycoddled me."

"You never gave him the chance and you never had a murderer after you," Nate muttered too low for his mother to hear. From the grin on Adeline's face, he knew she'd caught that comment. "Fine, Adeline can go to work, on the condition she accepts the protection offered, but Vianne stays here with you and Dad."

"I don't want to stay here. I want to go to work with Adeline. It's not fair," Vianne wailed.

Nate closed his eyes in exasperation. All he wanted was keep everyone safe.

"I don't care what you do or do not want, young lady. Nanny and Grandad have come all this way to spend time with us. I have to work today, so you get them all to yourself."

"But, Uncle Nate…"

"No buts. Maybe they'll do something fun with you." *I hope.*

His mother nodded. "We can do fun. How about we go shopping, Vianne? You look like you could do with some clothes that fit."

"OK. I'll go put my coat on."

Nate stifled a sigh and finished his coffee. He thumped the cup down on the table. There was nothing wrong with what Vianne was wearing and his mother knew it. He got up, praying he wouldn't say something he'd end up regretting. "I'll drop you off at work on my way in to the station, Adeline. But we need to leave now."

"Thanks. I'm ready to go."

****

The morning passed uneventfully. As tempting as it was, Adeline resisted the urge to send Nate a text saying 'told you so.'

Just after lunch, the sun vanished behind a bank of thick, ominous looking green-black clouds. The heavy oppressiveness grew and a severe storm warning was issued by the Met Office.

Adeline sent Mrs. Avon home and started around the building, disconnecting phone lines and electrical equipment.

Rain hit the windows as she closed them. Heading back into reception, she looked at PC Jones. "It's got really nasty out there. I might close up for the day." She moved to the door just as a huge flash of lightning flashed through the room.

The door opened and Vianne ran in, followed by her grandparents.

Adeline smiled at her. "Hello. This is a nice surprise."

"Can I stay here?" Vianne asked. "In the dry."

"We need to go to the bank and a couple of other places, and she'll get bored." Jeremiah smiled. "I don't want to put you out, but she insisted it would be all right. I wouldn't have gone against what Nate said if the weather hadn't suddenly become so disagreeable."

"Of course it's fine for her to stay here." She looked at Vianne. "Go and get the colors and books out. You can spread them all over the reception desk."

"Yay, thank you." Vianne grinned and ran off.

"Thank you. We won't be more than an hour or so."

"No problem. See you later."

Adeline sat next to Vianne.

Lightning flashed almost constantly with Vianne jumping soon after each flash. "Don't like thunder," she said.

"Mum says thunder is the devil throwing his boots down the stairs because he's in a mood," Adeline said. "But really, it's just the sound the lightning makes."

"It needs to shut up." Vianne scribbled hard on the paper. "Least you can't hear it."

DC Jones excused herself and headed out the back to the ladies.

Vianne dropped a pen on the floor and jumped under the counter to retrieve it.

The light over the door flashed, and as it opened a huge streak of lightning illuminated a figure standing there. He moved into the room, a strong scent of garlic preceding him.

Adeline's heart pounded in her chest, fear rose, catching her breath.

Ben huddled next to a cowering Vianne.

It must be thundering again. She glanced down, signing rapidly. "I need you to run and get Uncle Nate."

Vianne scrunched her face, signing back. "But it's thundering and raining."

Adeline signed back. "Please, Vianne. The bad man is here, and the phones aren't working."

Two hands landed on the counter, and the man leaned on the desk. The stench of garlic almost overpowered her, and she gagged.

His eyes were hauntingly familiar. He was a man she'd only met the once.

Susie's boyfriend. Storm.

But the eyes...she knew the eyes from her dreams and visions.

She sucked in a deep breath. "Can I help you?"

"Yes. You can die."

Petrified, Adeline swallowed hard. She signed frantically under the counter. "Go now. Take Ben. He and Jesus will protect you." She glanced down as Vianne tugged on her leg and shook her head. She signed again. "Please, go now."

Storm leaned over the counter. "What are you doing?"

"Run!" Adeline shouted.

Vianne darted from under the counter taking Ben's collar and leash.

Storm tried to grab her, pulling her hat from her head.

Vianne froze. "My hat. He took my hat."

Storm reached for her again, but Adeline knocked his arm away. "You wanted me, not the child."

PC Jones came back in. "What's going on?"

Storm turned as lightning flashed.

Adeline moved around the counter and grabbed Vianne, bundling her out the door. "Go and get Uncle Nate, now."

"But my hat…"

"Just go. Never mind your hat." She clipped on Ben's leash and gave it to Vianne as a hand gripped her, pulling her back into the room. She saw Vianne run off before Storm swung her around to face him.

PC Jones lay on the floor, eyes staring sightlessly, blood oozing from a head wound. Vianne's hat lay on the floor. A smoking gun waved in Adeline's face.

A hand flipped the closed sign over, locked the door, and pulled down the blind.

She looked into the hate-filled eyes.

Please, Lord, protect Vianne out there. Let her get to Nate safely.

She sucked in a deep breath. "What do you want with me?"

"It's time for some fun. And then you die. Just like all the others did. But you? You complete the pattern."

16

Nate sat at his desk, his mind focused on Adeline. His fingers traced a small photo of her. She'd objected when he took it, but he'd done it anyway. A diamond and amethyst ring that he'd slipped out and bought at lunchtime nestled in its box in his pocket.

How could things have changed so quickly? Last night he'd proposed and been on top of the world. The next moment everything had transformed into a nightmare.

He forced his mind to concentrate on the current situation. Dane was back in the interview room, interrogating the man they had assumed was the Herbalist. His fingerprints weren't in the system. They could find nothing on him at all. He gave his name only as Lightning. DI Welsh was tracking down traveler and hippy communities, but persuading the travelers to talk was worse than getting blood out of a stone.

Where there two killers working in tandem like pair of Jack-the-Rippers? Could one be a cop? The killer always seemed a step ahead of the police.

The phone rang, and he grabbed it. "Holmes."

"It's Constable Riggs on the front desk, sir. Could you come down immediately? There's a small child here by the name of Vianne asking for you."

"I'll be right there." Nate dropped the phone and ran from the office. He sped towards the fire door.

What was she doing here? And if she was alone, where were his parents? Had something happened to them?

The door hit the wall with a resounding thud, and echoed down the stairwell, as Nate took the stairs two at a time. Through another fire door and down the hallway to the main reception he ran, his heart pounding in his chest and a dozen worse case scenarios filling his brain.

Letting the door to the front office slam, he ignored Constable Riggs, his attention riveted to Vianne who sat on a plastic orange chair sobbing, Ben by her side, almost as if he were guarding her.

Something hit him with the force of ten sledgehammers, sending a portent of doom shuddering through him.

Vianne isn't wearing her hat.

He couldn't remember the last time she'd taken it off, never mind outside of the house. Why was she alone? Why was Ben here? Why had Ben left Adeline? Where were his parents?

Nate dropped to his knees and wrapped his arms around the distraught child. "It's OK, I'm here. You're soaked, pumpkin. What happened? I thought you were with Nanny and Grandad."

"I was. They left me with Adeline, while they went to the bank…"

He glanced around for Adeline. A chill of looming disaster filled him. Now he knew something was very, very wrong. His voice caught in his throat, questions tumbling from him in his need for information. "Where's Adeline? Where's your hat?"

"I lost it. The bad man has it."

"The bad man? What bad man?" He gently brushed the tears from Vianne's cheeks, desperately trying to calm her, so she could speak without sobbing. Ben licked her hands. "Vianne, where's Adeline?"

"Not here. The bad man's got her. At the doll hospital. She told me to come here where I'd be safe. She told me to find you."

Nate twisted around to the desk officer. "Get DS Philips and DI Welsh down here now."

As Constable Riggs lifted the phone, Dane rushed though, several uniformed officers behind him. "Nate, we've got to go. Shots fired at the doll—" He broke off seeing Vianne. "—At Datura," he amended. "CO19 are on the way."

Nate swallowed hard.

'Shots fired' was something else. CO19 or the Armed Response Unit would take time to arrive. Time Adeline might not have.

"Vianne, I need you to stay here." Nate turned to the desk. "Constable Riggs, please ring my parents. Here's the number. Tell them to stay here until I get back."

Vianne looked worried as more uniformed officers ran past. "What's happening?"

"We're going to go rescue Adeline." He kissed her cheek. Nate pulled out his handkerchief from his pocket. He pressed it into her hand. "Stay here. Constable Riggs will look after you until Grandad gets here. Keep this for me until I get back." He turned to the officer. "Don't let my parents leave. Put them in the interview room or something. They'll be safer here for now."

"Yes, sir."

Nate nodded and kissed the top of Vianne's head.

DI Welsh ran towards the door, barking orders on the phone as she ran. "CO19 are en route. Good. How did MI5 hear about this? If Agent Debone wants to attend that's fine, but I have jurisdiction here. Yes, I understand that. Nate, let's go."

Rain thudded against the window, lightning flashed, the thunder echoing.

"I'm right behind you. Keep an eye on Ben, pumpkin. He doesn't like storms."

"Jesus will look after us both. Is He going to look after you, too?"

"You bet. You, me, and Adeline. I'll see you soon. Remember I love you." Nate ran out after the others, praying hard.

****

Storm forced Adeline against his body, making her walk into the main ward in front of him. She tried to turn around. "If I can't see you, then I don't know what you're saying." The gun shoved harder into her side, and she swallowed hard.

Lord, if I'm going to die let it be swift, please. And be waiting for me when I arrive in heaven. Keep Vianne safe out there. And don't let Nate be filled with a desire for vengeance. Nate, I'm sorry things turned out this way. I should have listened to you.

An image of Nate with the white bandage over his nose flooded her mind. Instantly, she knew what she had to do. Adeline stamped hard on Storm's instep and pushed her elbow back sharply into his groin. As the man bent over, she flung her head back sharply into his face.

He let go and she fell to the floor. Pushing the pain in her hands and knees aside, she struggled upright and ran to the door. The lock jammed and her panic-stricken fingers made it as impossible to undo as a metal puzzle from a Christmas cracker.

"Please…" She screamed as someone grabbed her hair, yanking her backwards away from the door. Her heart pounded, breath came in gasps as he dragged her across the room and into her office. Forcing her into a chair, Storm pulled her hands behind her back tying them with the thin twine she used to reattach doll eyes.

He swung the chair around to face him, the gun pointed at her. Dark, hollow eyes burned into her, the same evil as before oozing from him.

As terrified as she was, Adeline wasn't going to show it. After all, no matter what this man had planned for her, God was in total control. She could feel His sheltering arms and hear His voice whispering peace to her. Perhaps if she kept the man talking, it would give Vianne time to get Nate.

She twisted her hands behind her, trying to loosen the bonds. The metal twine bit into her wrists, but the pain was good. It would keep her mind focused as she concentrated on the man in front of her. "What do you want?"

"I want you."

"Why me?"

"Why not you?" His eyes glinted and his lips curled into a snarl.

"I'm nothing special."

"Oh, but you are. It's all about you."

"Did you kill all those women and the Prime Minister just to get to me?"

"The Prime Minister was an accident. She got in the way. Literally." Storm laughed. "I'd just lined up the laser sight on you, and the stupid woman steps right in the way, blocking my line of sight. You had to die because you knew too much, and now you know who I am."

"But the police arrested someone, so the case is closed. If it wasn't you, then who is he?"

"My partner. I kill, and he dumps the bodies. He won't keep quiet, he doesn't know how to. He'll blab to save his own skin."

Adeline swallowed hard. "If you kill me, they'll know it wasn't him."

"You know it isn't him. You've known all along it isn't him. How?" His hand tightened on her throat, and she gagged then struggled to draw breath. "How. Did. You. Know?"

"Dreams. I dreamt all the murders and the smell…"

"Smell?" Storm's face contorted as lightning flashed.

"Garlic. Please, you're hurting me…"

The grip relaxed just a little as lightning flashed again. The lights flickered and went out. Storm twisted as blue lights flickered outside the windows.

Adeline recognized the curse on the man's lips and immediately turned it to a prayer. *Hallowed be Thy name.*

Her mobile phone on the desk lit up, and Storm nodded to it. "Answer it. Put it on speaker phone so I can hear."

She shrugged her shoulders. "My hands are tied behind my back. You'll have to do it. It doesn't work like that. I speak into it and get the replies as text. You can read the answers yourself. Hit the green button." He did so and held the phone to her. She leaned towards the mouthpiece. "Hello."

"This is Detective Inspector Welsh. Who am I

speaking to?"

"Adeline Monroe. I own the doll hospital."

"Are you all right, Adeline?"

"Not really," she replied honestly. After all, who'd be all right with twine cutting into their wrists and a gun in their face? Never mind the police officer lying in the other room.

"Is there someone there with you?"

"Yes."

"Who is it?"

Storm raised the gun. "You tell them and you die."

Adeline caught her breath. He must have forgotten the police could hear her and wasn't getting her speech as text. "I can't tell you. He killed the police officer, said he'd kill me. There's two of them, you caught the man who dumps the bod—" She broke off in a cry of pain, her head twisting with the force of the blow that she hadn't seen coming.

"Can I speak to him?"

Adeline managed to focus on Storm, who shook his head. Her vision blurred, and she could still see stars. She kept working on the knots behind her, her wrists slippery with blood. "He doesn't want to talk. He's reading everything you say."

"Reading?"

"I'm deaf. Whatever you say comes up on my screen as a text message."

The connection died.

****

Nate groaned as DI Welsh hung up.

"He can read everything we say. It's going to be impossible to communicate with her without him knowing."

"I did try to explain that before you rang. There is a way. If I can get to a window, I can sign to her…"

"And have this maniac take you out with his gun the minute he sees you?" The DI rolled her eyes, irritation in her voice. "I don't think so. He killed Denise—"

Nate staggered back as if punched in the gut. "What?"

"Adeline said Denise was dead, and she has no reason to lie. She also said there were two of them and we only caught one. She then cried out in pain. And it didn't sound like it was the first time he hurt her."

"Then we go in." Nate stood up straight. "I'm not letting him hurt her again."

DI Welsh looked at him, with a mix of frustration and exasperation. "My hands are tied. I can't risk anyone else until CO19 get here. I especially can't risk someone who's personally involved. Once CO19 arrive, then we'll just go in hard and fast. You can wait here."

"Oh, no, there's no way I'm just going to sit and wait. I may be personally involved here, but I'm working. You assigned me to protect her. I'm trying to do that." Nate turned away. This was taking too long.

Lord, I have to get in there. Keep her safe, be with her.

He looked at Dane. "What about around the back?"

"Yeah there's a way in there. Jas jokingly called it the tradesman's entrance."

Nate turned to DI Welsh. "Guv, please. At least let us go and look."

"Just be careful. Don't go in without telling me

first."

Nate jerked his head in response and ran off with Dane. He pulled up as Agent Debone's car drew to a halt.

Agent Debone jumped out and strode over to Nate. "What's going on? I thought you wanted minimal back up not the whole shooting match? I just got a call saying CO19 are on the way."

"It's the Herbalist. We only caught his partner. We have one officer down. Adeline's been taken hostage. We're checking out another way in. The guy has already hurt her once. I'm not going to let him do it again."

"Count me in. Is Vianne in there?"

"No, she's at the station. She managed to get out and raise the alarm. Are you armed?"

Debone nodded curtly. He unbuttoned his jacket to reveal a shoulder holster. "Yes, I am."

"Come. We're going around the back."

The men ran into the alley. A padlocked gate and a six-foot tall fence stood between them and the doll hospital. The pouring rain soaked into their coats as they pulled themselves over the fence, dropping quietly into the backyard.

Hunching down to avoid being seen by anyone inside the building, the men ran to the door. Dane pulled aside the plant pot and picked up the spare key.

"That's not very safe," Nate said bluntly. "Didn't you ever tell them that?"

"Jas said it was for emergency use only. I reckon breaking in to rescue a hostage counts as an emergency, don't you?"

"Well, we are the emergency services, so yeah, I think it does."

"Is this really the time for inane chit-chat?" Agent Debone asked.

"It's something we've always done. It relieves the tension. Ready?"

Dane quietly unlocked door, as Agent Debone slid his gun from its holster and pulled back the safety. Nate lifted his radio to tell the Guv and get permission to go in.

A shot came from inside.

Nate's heart leapt. All conscious thought left. He reacted purely on instinct. "Shots fired. Going in."

17

The phone rang again, flashing its light just as the metal twine binding her slid to the floor. Her wrists were now slick with blood, and pins and needles shot down her fingers. Adeline took a deep breath, leaning towards the microphone. "Hello?" Lightning split the room as she answered.

Storm brandished the gun in her face, leaning across to speak into phone.

Adeline took her chance, everything Nate had taught her filling her mind. She caught hold of his wrist and twisted the gun in his hand. She felt the vibration and flash as it went off.

Storm's hand came up, gripping her.

Adeline kicked as he pulled her back against him, his arm around her throat. She threw her head back, feeling a satisfying crunch as something broke under the force of the blow. She bent forwards, and gripping Storm's arm around her throat, tugged him over her shoulder onto the desk.

There was another flash, and she fell to the ground, as something hit her arm. Pain flooded her.

Storm leaned over her, blood and venomous curse words falling from his lips. The gun pressed against her head, and she knew in that instant she could die.

Storm jerked, and his eyes widened. Then he fell to one side, his grip on her vanishing.

Not sure what happened, Adeline froze. Her gaze

slid to the man standing over her, gun pointing downwards.

Agent Debone?

"How…?" she began, her voice fading.

A hand turned her face to the left. Nate's concerned gaze met hers.

"Nate…" She tried to sit up.

"Don't move, not until someone checks you over."

"I'm fine," she insisted, pushing against the floor. She gasped in pain, clutching her arm.

"You're bleeding and you're in pain. That's as far from fine as you can get."

Strong arms folded around her, and she leaned into Nate. She glanced at Storm, who was face down and in cuffs. "It's nothing, been through worse."

Dane and Agent Debone hauled Storm to his feet. Blood poured from his nose and his arm.

"That's some right hook you have, Miss Monroe," Agent Debone told her. "You've broken his nose."

"It's a talent I have, and it wasn't my hand."

Nate laughed. "You head-butted him?"

Adeline nodded, her gaze swiveling between the two men as they spoke.

"I should never have taught you that one."

"It did save my life. He's the Herbalist. He kills the women. The man you have in custody moves the bodies afterwards."

Dane froze, his fists clenching. He took a step towards him.

Storm grinned. "Yeah, the Herbalist is what the papers call me. Much better than anything I could have come up with myself."

"You killed my wife."

"Yeah. What of it?"

Nate moved over to him. "Dane?"

Dane shook his head. "Don't worry, Nate. I'm not going to hit him. He's not worth it. The courts can deal with him."

Adeline watched the exchange. "Nate? Is Vianne safe?"

"She's at the station with Ben. You know she came without her hat?"

"He took it away, trying to stop her from leaving. She really found you? On her own? Without a hat?"

"Yeah. One very brave little girl. I will let her know you're all right."

"Only if I come, too."

More police ran into the building, and Nate turned and conferred with his boss. Then he turned back to her. "OK. Come on. You need to be seen by the police surgeon at the station."

****

Nate stood in doorway with Dane, half listening to the Guv as he watched Adeline and Vianne talking.

Adeline had given her statement and had her arm bandaged by the police surgeon. A bullet burn, all it needed was dressing. Things could have been so much worse, and he was so incredibly grateful to the Lord that they got there when they did. A litany of praise ran through his mind every few seconds. *Thank You, God. Thank You for saving those I love.*

DI Welsh touched his arm. "Nate, are you all right?"

"I'm fine."

She smiled. "Then take them home. We'll see you in the morning."

"Are you sure?"

Dane nodded. "I'll start the paperwork. They need you more than we do right now."

"Thanks. See you tomorrow." He moved closer to the girls, able to hear what they were saying.

"I'm glad you're OK." Vianne's voice, although quiet, was stronger.

"I'm glad you're OK, too. You're a clever girl to go get help. And without a hat."

"Jesus is way better than a hat. He does the same thing only from the inside."

"Yes, He does. Way, way better than a hat. He looked after me, too."

Nate hunkered down in front of them, taking one of their hands in each of his. "Ready to go home?"

Adeline nodded. "More than ready."

Vianne nodded, her hand still clasped in Adeline's fingers.

Nate leaned over and kissed Adeline. "Then let's go home. We have a wedding to plan. I almost lost you today. I don't want to wait longer than I have to before I make you my wife."

"Then how does February sound? That'll give your mum six months to get used to the idea."

"Sounds good to me."

Vianne looked from one to the other. "Did you say wedding? Are you getting married?"

"We sure are. I asked her last night."

"Yay!" Vianne's shriek of delight almost deafened him and she hugged them both. Then she pulled back and winked at Adeline. "I'd moved you to the top of the list, anyway."

"What list?" Nate asked.

Vianne giggled. "The list of women you could

marry so I can have an auntie."

He ruffled her hair. "You, child, are incorrigible."

Confusion flooded her small face. "Is that a good thing?"

Adeline laughed. "Yes, it's a good thing." She hugged her and held Nate's gaze over the top of Vianne's head. "It is *really* over now, isn't it?"

Nate nodded. "Yes. It's really over."

18

Six months later.

Nate didn't think it was possible to be this nervous. Not since Adeline had been held at gun point had he felt like this. A dozen thoughts dashed though his mind, each scenario worse than the preceding one.

Why couldn't the snow have held off for one more day? What if she's too late and we have to postpone the wedding? What if the car crashes on the way to the church? What if she gets stuck in all that snow out there? What if she changes her mind, or gets cold feet? What if…?

He glanced at Dane, his best man. He fiddled with his tie and pulled at his jacket.

What if she doesn't come at all?

"You look like a cat on a hot tin roof," Dane chuckled. "Relax, she'll be here. Of course, she'll be wearing pink pajamas, riding six white horses, and we'll all have chicken and dumplings when she comes, but yeah, she'll turn up. For some reason that defies logic, that woman loves you to bits, as Vianne would say." He raised an eyebrow. "Not even a hint of a smile?"

Nate shook his head and checked his watch. Something must have happened. She should be here by now. He peered over his shoulder at the full church. This might be the worst, most embarrassing day of his life. He just knew it. He loved her so much, had opened himself to her in ways he had never dared do with anyone, not even Dane.

Corrine, Adeline's mother, waved at him from where she sat next to David, Adeline's father, on the end of the front pew. The stroke he'd had on the cruise had almost killed him and left him confined to a wheelchair. Unable to walk or speak right now, he communicated via sign language. As far as Adeline knew, Mark was walking her up the aisle in his place, with David planning on giving her away himself.

But he, David and Mark had hatched a plan.

God, please, keep her safe out there. Don't let anything have happened to her, today of all days—not that I'd want anything to have happened to her any other day. You know what I mean. We've planned this, longed for this day for so long. And even despite her father's stroke, we managed to get this far.

Nate rechecked his watch and then sighed as he realized less than a minute had passed. He turned his attention back to Dane. His stomach twisted and his heart broke. "I don't think she's coming. I should say something."

Dane gave him a pat on the shoulder, holding him still. "Give her a bit longer. The roads are awful. It took us ages to get here as it is, everyone was late arriving. And they're coming from further."

"She's forty minutes late. Everyone's talking. I—"

"Let me go ring Mark. Do you have his number?"

"I don't have my phone. It's packed because I didn't think I'd need it."

"OK."

"I'll go and ask her mum to ring." Nate shoved his hands into his pockets. "She's bound to have her phone with her."

Corrine came over to them.

Nate smiled nervously. "I was just coming to see you."

She smiled. "Mark just rang. They are on the way, but got stuck in a snow drift."

Nate groaned and pushed his hands through his hair. "Noooo."

"It's fine. They've called for help and will be here as soon as they can."

"Maybe I should get over there and—"

"And get stuck as well?" Dane asked. "Just sit and wait and she'll be here before you know it."

"That's easy for you to say."

Dane put a hand on his shoulder. "Then sit down and we'll pray for her safety and the rescue crews."

He nodded and glanced over at David.

David held his gaze and slowly signed at him.

Nate smiled. "Thank you," he signed back.

"What did he say?" Dane asked.

"Do not be afraid appears in the Bible three hundred and sixty-six times. That's one for every day of the year."

Dane smiled. "There you go then. Don't be afraid, she'll be here."

He nodded and glanced towards the back of the church to check on Vianne. She sat in her bridesmaids dress on one of the chairs by the welcome desk, swinging her feet. He caught her eye. "Love you," he signed.

She winked at him and signed back. "Love you, too."

****

Adeline sat in the limousine, shivering in her

wedding dress, despite the heat being blasted through the car. Snow lay seven inches deep in places on the roads and the car was stuck. Rescue services were on the way, but she had no idea how long they'd take to get here. She was late for her own wedding. And she was never late for anything. And she didn't want to start being late now.

She turned away from the snow-covered landscape, and heaved a sigh. "Nate will think I'm not coming."

"I already rang Mum. She'll tell him what happened and that we'll get there."

She ran her hands over her white velvet gown. Her tiara of roses and diamonds lay flat against her blonde hair, the veil cascading over her shoulders. On her lap lay her bouquet of red and white roses. They had cost a fortune for a February wedding, but one she deemed worth it.

Ben sat next to her, a red velvet collar around his neck. He licked her fingers, and she petted him. "What if she doesn't tell him? What if we never make it?"

Mark gave her a smile. "You worry far too much. You'll get there. Do you want me to ring the church again and tell them we are still coming?"

"No." She signed emphatically as she spoke. "Why keep calling?"

"Pfft, woman. He'll be out of his mind with worry. How much longer?" he asked the driver, receiving a shrug in response. Mark touched Adeline's hand. "Back in a tick, going to ring the church." He exited the car and pulled out his phone.

Adeline shook her head and looked down at Ben. "If he thinks pacing in the snow will help, it won't. It'll just ruin his suit. Why did it have to snow last night? It could have held off for one more day."

She gazed out of the window at the snow. *Lord, you know how much I want to marry Nate. We've come through so much to get this far. Please, let me get there.*

Four minutes later Mark climbed back into the car, bringing a blast of frigid air in with him. "I called the church. Pastor Jack said he'd let Nate know." He grinned. "He doesn't have his phone on him, either."

Adeline rolled her eyes. "And where am I supposed to put a phone? I don't have a handbag. At least he has a pocket in his jacket." She smirked at him. "I suppose I could have stuck it inside my bra along with my purse and my tissues."

"There's no need for that, sis. 'Sides, I called the cavalry. We'll be out of here in no time."

Adeline looked at him wondering what he had planned. "Mark?" He shook his head. She wrapped her arms round herself, shivering. "I should have worn a coat."

Mark slid out of his frock coat and wrapped it around her shoulders.

She closed her eyes, tears forming behind her lashes. "I'm sorry, Nate." She loved him so much, wanted so desperately to be his wife, and it was not going to happen.

A few minutes later, Mark tapped her arm. She opened her eyes and looked at him, then past him to the window. Her eyes widened as she saw a huge Humvee parked next to the limo.

"Mark, what have you done?"

Mark smiled. "I told you we'd get there." He picked her up as she got out of the car and lifted her into the Humvee. "I simply pulled in a few favors at work and told them that my sister was stuck in the snow and going to be late to her own wedding. The boys were all too happy to help." He climbed in behind her. "Wish I could see Nate's face when this pulls up outside the church."

****

Nate kept pacing. He'd tried sitting and praying, sitting and reading the order of service. He'd even tried talking to his parents and parents-in-law to be, but nothing calmed his nerves. Since he'd got Mark's message that everything was under control, his heart had lightened. Although worried about his bride stuck in the snow, he knew she'd be here eventually. But still he couldn't settle.

Loud engine sounds echoed through the church. He turned, half wanting to see what was happening, the other half of him reasoning people would think he was leaving if he did.

Pastor Jack stuck his head into the chapel and gave Nate the thumbs up. "She's here," he mouthed.

No longer caring what anyone thought, Nate ran down the aisle. He burst through the doors and skidded to a halt on the steps. His jaw dropped at the sight of the Humvee parked outside the church. "What?"

"It's something," Pastor Jack said.

Nate saw Adeline being lifted bodily from the Humvee and carried up the path to the church doors by a soldier in uniform. The photographer caught every moment.

Adeline smiled at the soldier, not letting go. Her train was slung over her arm so it wouldn't drag in the snow. "Thank you so much."

"You're welcome. Anything for the Colonel's sister."

Another soldier put Ben on the steps beside her.

Nate moved to her side. "Adeline, what happened? Are you all right?" he asked, looking in amazement at the Humvee.

"The car got stuck in a snow drift. Mark called the base, and this is the rescue team. I had to get here. I love you."

He pulled her into his arms, lifted her veil and kissed her soundly. "And I love you. You look amazing."

Pastor Jack coughed. "Shall we make a start?"

Nate reluctantly let go of Adeline. He kissed her cheek and winked. "I'll see you in a minute," he signed. "Don't be late."

Adeline's laugh filled him with joy. "Oh, I think I'm way beyond late. I could always race you up the aisle. Or walk up it with you."

"Don't you dare. Give me two minute's head start." He turned to find a crowd of family and friends gaping at the Humvee. "We're ready now," He announced.

Everyone rushed back to their seats.

Nate followed them into the church. He grinned at Dane who'd stayed in the church with the girls. "The army rescued her, brought her here in a Humvee."

"Wow. That girl of yours knows how to make an entrance."

"She sure does." He moved over to David. "She's here. Are you ready?"

"You treat her right," he signed slowly.

"I promise," Nate signed back.

"Then I'm ready."

"Let's get you down there." He wheeled David to the bottom of the aisle, leaving him just inside the door, where Adeline wouldn't see him until the last minute.

Returning to the front of the church, he stood by the platform. The organ started playing Saint Saëns's *Organ Concerto in C Major*. Adeline had chosen it because it was Nate's favorite piece of classical music.

Vianne and Ben walked the aisle together, followed by Dane's girls, scattering rose petals on the way.

****

Adeline smoothed down her dress. She could feel the vibrations of the organ increase and knew it was time for her entrance.

Mark grinned at her. "Ready?"

She nodded and tried to take his arm

"No, sis." He took her hand and led her to the door. "Dad wanted to do it. I'm pushing him, he's holding your hand."

Tears filled her eyes and her heart leapt into her throat. "Oh…"

David beamed up at her, his shaking hand extended towards her.

She knelt beside the chair. "Dad," she signed. "I had no idea."

"I want to do this," he signed slowly. "Shall we?"

She kissed his cheek and stood up, tears streaming down her face. Transferring her flowers to her left hand, she gripped her father's hand tightly with her right. She glanced back at Mark, standing behind the wheelchair and he nodded to her.

Adeline smiled through the tears and took her first step towards her new life.

****

As the music grew louder, Nate's nerves grew. He risked a glance over his shoulder and his heart swelled with pride.

Adeline, her father, and brother slowly made their way to the front of the church. She kept her eyes on Nate the whole time, a huge grin on her face, despite the way her shoulders shook and tears streamed down her face.

He had never seen her look so radiant. *Thank you, Lord, for bringing us safely to this day. Be with us now and in the years to come.*

"Did you know about this?" she asked, taking her place.

"Mark, David, and I planned it several weeks ago. Your Dad wanted to do this so very much."

"Thank you."

Pastor Jack led them through the legal bits they had to say, then smiled at David. Slowly he signed the words he'd been taught as he spoke them aloud. "Who gives this woman to be married to this man?"

David beamed at him and raised a thumb's up before signing back, "I do." He then put Adeline's hand into Nate's.

"Nate and Adeline have written their own vows," Pastor Jack said.

Nate took her hand and turned to face her. He let go of her hand and slowly signed, speaking at the same time. "I, Nathaniel James Holmes, take you Adeline Stacey Monroe to be my wife, my partner in life and my one true love. I will cherish our friendship and love you today, tomorrow, and forever. I will trust you and honor you. I will laugh with you and cry with you. I will love you faithfully through the best and the worst, through the difficult and the easy. What may come I will always be there. As I have given you my hand to hold, so I give you my life to keep."

Adeline smiled at him. She also signed and spoke. "I, Adeline Stacey Monroe, take you Nathaniel James Holmes, to be my husband, my partner in life and my one true love. I will cherish our friendship and love you today, tomorrow, and forever. I will trust you and honor you. I will laugh with you and cry with you. I will love you faithfully through the best and the worst, through the difficult and the easy. What may come I will always be there. As I have given you my hand to hold, so I give you my life to keep."

They exchanged rings, and Nate pulled her into his arms and kissed her. Once the applause from the congregation ended, he broke the kiss. "Hello, Mrs. Holmes." He signed as he spoke.

She smiled and signed back. "I like the way that looks." She changed to speech. "Just do me one favor. Please, promise me that you won't call our first son Sherlock. No matter who begs you to? He won't thank you for it, and neither will I."

Nate paused for a moment and then laughed. "No fear of that." His eyes twinkled with love before turning to face their friends and family—his wife at his side.